# SONATA #1 *for*

## Riley Red

# Also by Phoebe Stone

∽

*All the Blue Moons at the Wallace Hotel*

*Go Away, Shelley Boo!*

*What Night Do the Angels Wander?*

*When the Wind Bears Go Dancing*

# SONATA #1 *for*

# Riley Red

*by*

# Phoebe Stone

**LITTLE, BROWN AND COMPANY**

**New York** ♪ An AOL Time Warner Company

First Edition

The characters and events portrayed in this book are fictitious. Any similarity
to real persons, living or dead, is coincidental and not intended by the author.

The author is grateful for permission to reprint the following:
"Blowin' in the Wind." Copyright © 1962 by Warner Bros., Inc. Copyright renewed
1990 by Special Rider Music. All rights reserved. International copyright secured.
Reprinted by permission. "Girl of the North Country." Copyright © 1963 by Warner
Bros., Inc. Copyright renewed 1991 by Special Rider Music. All rights reserved.
International copyright secured. Reprinted by permission.

Library of Congress Cataloging-in-Publication Data

Stone, Phoebe.
    Sonata #1 for Riley Red / by Phoebe Stone. — 1st ed.
        p.   cm.
    Summary: Thirteen-year-old Rachel and her "outcast" friends
struggle to come to terms with unresolved emotional traumas while trying
to rescue a neglected zoo elephant in a small town outside of Boston.
    ISBN 0-316-99041-8
    [1. Emotional problems — Fiction. 2. Family problems — Fiction.
3. Animal welfare — Fiction. 4. Elephants — Fiction. 5. Piano — Fiction.
6. Apartment houses — Fiction. 7. Boston (Mass.) — Fiction.] I. Title:
Sonata Number One for Riley Red. II. Title.

PZ7.S879 So 2003
[Fic] — dc21                                                          2002036846

10 9 8 7 6 5 4 3 2 1

Q-FF

Printed in the United States of America

The text was set in Cochin, and the display type is Gigi.

*For David and Ethan, yet again, because I love you.*
*And for the elephants.*

# Acknowledgments

Thank you to my mother, the incomparable Ruth Stone, for her encouragement and for listening to this manuscript over the phone many, many times. Thank you to Maria Modugno for her love and support, and for making the book a book. Thank you to Amy Hsu for her gentleness and care, and to Marian Young for being Marian Young. Thank you to Alyssa Morris for designing with such ease. Thank you to my dear, sweet friends Yvette Feig and Bob Murray for reading this book early on, and to Karin Gottshall for her poetic suggestions.

# SONATA #1 *for*

## Riley Red

*Chapter One*

Here's a list of some of the things my friend Desmona wants to do tomorrow.

One: Have a picnic in the graveyard in Harvard Square on her mother's grave, like they do in Mexico on the Day of the Dead. But everyone agrees that's completely morbid.

Two: Go to the pound in Somerville and bring home eight cats that would otherwise be finished, kaput, and deliver them to all the tenants in my building, 87 Brattle Street (a block from Harvard Square). Last time we did that, we put the cats in the old Victorian elevator and went around to all the apartments. We gave one to Mrs. Ethel Elgar, who was quite pleased. Another one went to

Woolsey's father, Sergeant Pontiac, even though he's allergic, and we gave the cutest tiger kitten to the ninety-two-year-old Butterfield sisters in apartment 6C. But my piano teacher, Mr. Krimms, had to return the big yellow tabby we gave him because it sat by his fish tank all day and he thought it was disturbing the equilibrium in the water. So I ended up with another cat, and I've taken in three already.

So we say no to Desmona's idea about visiting the pound. Not just no, but absolutely no.

That's when Riley suggests we drive to Walden Pond tomorrow for a swim, and suddenly everyone starts smiling.

Before I go any further, let me explain a few things about my friend Desmona. First of all, we are both in Mr. Burns's class, English 152. We both have long hair, only mine is usually brushed and pinned back with a barrette, but there *is* no barrette that will contain my friend Desmona's hair. Even though we are both only thirteen, she wears dark, smudged eye shadow *underneath* her eyes, making her look like something out of a 1920s silent movie. But Desmona has never been silent, and she can do things that the rest of us can't even attempt, partly because of her brother, Riley, and that car of his. They can go anywhere they want, all over Cambridge, all over Boston. A lot of the time, there's room for us to go along, Woolsey and me and Darcy. Sometimes we even go out to Walden Pond just to skip stones and talk.

We can also drive to the local pound in Somerville, which we did last week, with Riley at the wheel and me and Woolsey in the backseat holding cardboard boxes in our arms, getting ready to save that week's collection of cats.

"If we don't," Desmona said, sitting backward in the front seat, looking at me and Woolsey, "if we don't, they'll all die, and it's cruel and wrong. We *have* to save them."

I just can't begin to explain the feeling of being thirteen years old and riding in Riley's sports car around Harvard Square—Riley's red curls, Desmona's hair blowing all over the place like a dark cloud in the wind, crowds of people milling around the Coop and magazine stands, everybody looking up at us, astonished at Riley's red hair, astonished at Desmona's dark painted eyes and the little red car.

"Woolsey, you know you have room for another cat, and three is a better number than two," said Desmona that day.

"Yeah, but my father's allergic," said Woolsey, looking uncomfortable.

We gave Woolsey the name Woolsey because his real name is Alfred Pontiac (like the car), and Desmona was sure his name had something to do with eighth- and ninth-graders not liking him. It's true that when Woolsey used to be Alfred Pontiac, hardly anyone would have anything to do with him. But things changed after Desmona discovered him one day and decided to add him to the group. He was eating lunch all by himself in a far corner of the cafeteria, hiding behind a science-fiction book and stuffing himself with peanut butter cookies.

"I think you'll do better with a name like Woolsey," said Desmona later, as they were walking through Harvard Square. "It's warm and fuzzy and friendly. It's everything that Alfred Pontiac is not."

This afternoon I'm at Desmona's house on Brattle Street. It is huge and elegant and full of dark polished wood and books, fine paintings and antique heirlooms. It has a hall tree with a mirror on it that reminds me of a queen's throne; it sits in the main hall at the bottom of a sweeping "darling-how-are-you" kind of staircase. Sometimes Desmona will greet me from the top. She'll throw her hand like a fan up to her mouth and say, "But, darling, how good to see you."

And I'll say, "Desmona, cut the crap," and she'll giggle.

Today Desmona is sitting in her room at her tiny electric sewing machine, orange silk-velvet fabric flying out behind her as the machine roars along. "This is going to be my best outfit yet," says Desmona to me. "I already made a little turban to match. I'm going to wear it tomorrow night when we pick my father up at the airport if I can just finish this skirt." Desmona is stepping on the pedal of the sewing machine, going 120 miles per hour. I swear I can see smoke. There are chunks of shimmery orange fabric all over everything and bright-colored spools of thread tossed around, making her rug look like a crazy game board. (Like a 2 A.M. Monopoly game with Riley amassing great fortunes and me and Desmona miserable and practically homeless, limping around the board.)

Desmona never uses a pattern when she sews. She conceives of the dresses as if in a dream, so they always come out kind of lopsided. She sees them and races after them with her slipshod scissors and a lot of estimation.

"My guess is that my stepmother probably won't let me wear this," says Des. "She'll say, 'But it hangs so crooked,' or 'Your arm barely fits in the sleeve. You're cutting off your circulation. It won't do. Your father will never approve.' I haven't seen Daddy for three months, and I want him to *notice* me. But he probably won't. Nothing I ever do startles him or causes him to take his eyes off *her*. A long time ago, she used to be Miss West Germany, you know."

"No, I didn't know that," I say, looking up at a framed newspaper clipping on the wall above Desmona. It says, SOCIALITE DROWNS IN WALDEN POND.

"My mother wasn't a socialite," says Desmona. "She was a poet, and I would have rescued her if I had known how—if I hadn't been such a child. You know, I think people are put on earth to do extraordinary things—even children. At least each of us is meant to do *one* extraordinary thing. Don't you think?" Desmona stops the sewing machine and puts the velvet orange turban on her head.

"I never really thought about it," I say.

"I suppose the principal will have a catatonic fit if I wear this to school," says Desmona.

"That hasn't stopped you so far, Des," I say, lying

back on the floor, looking up at the ceiling. The lights from Desmona's Christmas tree blink red and green and blue in the far corner. It's May. The air outside the window is fragrant with the smell of mock orange blossoms.

Air like this makes me think of Chopin, especially when the wind blows or when it rains. That's when I love to be playing the piano. That's when I long to write a piece of music of my own, but I never can. It's been two years since I've been able to write anything at all. Maybe today it will happen when I'm practicing. Maybe today a song will come to me.

Desmona says, "One extraordinary thing could make a person's life special. Anything could happen after that. It wouldn't matter. Nothing would matter but that one great thing."

Des is still in the orange turban, and she's looking out the window. She's the only person I know who can cry on call. Anytime she needs them to, tears go streaming down her cheeks. She gets all the good parts in the plays at school—all the crying, melting, burned-at-the-stake parts.

"Look at this article," she says, opening a drawer and pulling out a sheet of newspaper. "Look at this photograph of this sweet little child with an ice cream. The caption reads, *Spring has come to Lockwell,*

7

*Massachusetts.* It's a cute picture, but look a little closer. Look behind in the background. There's this elephant. It's chained up. It's chained up on a short chain. It's being mistreated. Take a closer look. Look how dumpy the park looks. Can you believe how people treat animals? And they think nothing of it."

A red cardinal streaks past the window behind her, darting through the mock orange bushes. Desmona has a yard full of cardinals that she feeds (five pairs at least). She also has a house full of cats that were saved from the pound split seconds before death. One of those cats comes up to me now and leans against my skirt, purring.

"Desmona, how can you have both cats and birds at the same time?" I ask her.

And Desmona says, "Life is two-sided. How can I love my brother, Riley, so much and hate him so desperately, too? Oh, crap." Desmona jumps up suddenly, and the orange fabric on her lap drops to the floor. "I forgot something. I left my book bag in Henry's garden. I'll be right back. No, have Riley drive over and get me in ten minutes."

By "Henry" Desmona means Henry Wadsworth Longfellow. His great lit-up, stately yellow house sits two blocks from here on Brattle Street. Desmona practically lives in his garden there, reading his poetry and thinking.

Desmona leaps out of the room and goes crashing down the staircase. Her stepmother, Gretchen, is at the bottom of the stairs. She says, "Desmona, slow down and walk with more grace, please. Are you a horse or a young lady?" And Desmona starts neighing and whinnying and snorting. Gretchen is always after Desmona about her descending-the-stairs technique. "Quit plunging," she says. "There isn't a swimming pool at the bottom, you know." Often, Gretchen makes Desmona walk across the room with Webster's complete dictionary on her head to encourage balance and grace.

Now I can hear Desmona whinnying and galloping across the rolling lawn outside. She's really overdoing this horse bit. At the same time, I can hear Gretchen downstairs snapping doors shut, one after another.

I climb the stairs to the third floor in Desmona's house to a big room at the top, where there's a large green pool table with orange and yellow and red billiard balls scattered across it. When I get up there, Riley is lying under the pool table wearing blue jeans, a T-shirt, and that crazy tuxedo jacket of his. He is barefoot. I can see his long freckled feet sticking out from under the table. He's reading the poem *To a Skylark*. He's always reading poetry aloud.

*Like a high-born maiden*
*In a palace tower,*
*Soothing her love-laden*
*Soul in secret hour*

"Shelley is great," he says to me. "Mr. Burns, English 152. Have you had him yet?"

"Yeah," I say, "Desmona and I are both in his class."

"He's the only teacher worth having in the whole of Cambridge High and Latin," says Riley. "'*Like a high-born maiden / In a palace tower*' ... that's got to be Christina Talbot with her floating long blond hair. Shelley must have known Christina Talbot," he says, sitting up. "Christina Talbot," he calls out, "my Skylark!"

I turn away and look out the window. All of Cambridge is below — churches, gardens, walled-in yards, and apple and cherry trees in bloom.

"Does she go to our school?" I ask, hiding my

face in the curtain of my hair, hiding my eyes in a curtain of shadow.

"Nope," says Riley. "She did last year though. She goes to Commonwealth now. She's gone. *Poof,* drowned in the river of time. She was in my biology class last year, but the thing is, I got in trouble because Des and I broke into that classroom and set all the frogs free that Mr. Hodge was planning to gas and put in formaldehyde. We drove all thirty of them over to the Charles River and set them free. That was a great day, especially for Desmona. Something like that brings her to life. She loves to be rescuing things. You know what I mean?"

"I do," I say, thinking of myself, thinking of Woolsey and Darcy and all the others.

"But I wasn't very popular in that class after that. Christina was up in the front row with her floating long yellow hair, and I was put at the back of the class. Then I had to go to detention hall for three months because of those thirty frogs. I hope they're happy raising families in the Charles River, because I lost my chance with Christina Talbot." He gets to his feet, picks up a pool cue, and pockets an orange five ball. "Nah," he goes on, "she's at Commonwealth, but I drive by her house all the time—at least once a day."

"Still?" I say.

"Still," he says.

Riley aims his cue, shoots, and the black ball spins into a pocket. "Bingo," says Riley. "I'm done."

I follow Riley down the wide, curving staircase. Downstairs in the open library off the main hall is Desmona and Riley's stepmother. She sits on a delicate sofa in the dim glow of a Tiffany lamp. She's knitting white angora baby booties. Her needles move like lightning in her hands. As we walk by, she looks up for a second as if she's raising a window shade and then pulling it back down.

Outside, Riley tosses his keys from one hand to the other like a juggler. I run a little to keep up with him, crossing the formal yard heading toward the car, which is parked in the circular driveway. Then Riley throws the keys up in the air, opens the car door, jumps in, and catches the keys just before they fall in his lap. He looks at me and smiles. "She wanted us to call her 'Mama,'" says Riley, starting the engine, "but we couldn't. Not so soon. She just happened too quickly. Especially for Desmona. We just couldn't."

Riley has a reel-to-reel tape recorder on the floor

of his car. He punches it on and this new folk-singer Bob Dylan sings to us with his scratchy voice. Sometimes it wavers out of tune, but that only seems to make the songs more heartfelt and real. As we ride off in the tiny little low-to-the-ground sports car, I feel like the wind itself rushing along, because never in all my thirteen years have I ever seen anything like this Riley McKarroll.

We pull up in front of Henry Wadsworth Longfellow's house. Desmona is sitting on a little garden bench, playing with that squirrel she's been feeding since he was little. He's wild for potato chips. Desmona pulls one out of the bag, and the squirrel grabs it. Sometimes he will run up her arm to her shoulder, with his jittery head turning this way and that. "Come on, you silly thing, climb. Climb," Desmona says.

Desmona doesn't see us now. We sit there in the car, Riley with his arms crossed at the top of the steering wheel, his head tilted back. "Look at that," says Riley. "She's so involved with that crazy squirrel, she doesn't even see us." Then, with a nervous jerky motion, the squirrel runs off into one of the blossoming cherry trees above. Desmona sits there, staring down at her sandals. Suddenly she looks small and sad, sitting all alone in that famous man's great big garden.

∽

"How long have you two idiots been here?" says Desmona, walking toward the car, holding on to the strap of her Harvard book bag, which is over her shoulder and on her back the way the Cliffy girls carry theirs. She kicks her foot, and her leather sandal flies up and falls into the car ahead of her on the backseat. She does the other sandal, too, but that one misses the mark and hits Riley on the right shoulder.

Riley says, "Good shot, Des. You just made the team."

Des climbs into the backseat without opening the door. "Ouch, crap," she says. "I think I just ripped my skirt."

Riley revs the motor, and we zip away from Henry Wadsworth Longfellow's house and curve down Brattle Street.

"What are you in such a hurry for?" Desmona calls into the wind.

"We're driving by the Skylark's house—Christina Talbot's." Riley looks over his shoulder at Desmona.

"Riley," says Desmona, "give it up."

"You guys are just little kids. You don't understand," says Riley. Riley's older than us. He's sixteen, but he's so tall that some guy at the Fogg Art Museum last week thought he was eighteen. We had gone there to see the Joan of Arc painting. Desmona *has* to visit that painting every week, once a week. She says that painting is her lifeblood. She says if she doesn't visit it, she might die.

"I'm not a little kid, Riley, and neither is Rachel. You're the one who's acting childish. This woman you're in love with doesn't even know you exist," says Desmona (I like the way Desmona calls Christina a *woman* instead of a *girl*).

"Oh, I wouldn't say that," says Riley, smiling, curly red hair blowing all around, his tiger yellow-green eyes landing on me for a minute and then on Des and then back to the road ahead, which is lined with garden walls of ivy. We turn onto a series of backstreets and wind up a little hill. Riley parks the car, and we sit under this big kneeling, bowing tree, which Desmona says is a chestnut.

"They've been trying to cut these trees down, because: *(a)* they're messy and *(b)* they fall over in windstorms, but I think they're beautiful," says Desmona.

"Shh," says Riley. "Let's be quiet now. She could come home at any minute."

We sit there in silence for a long time, ten to fifteen minutes, but we never see Christina Talbot. I have to pee, and Desmona has fallen asleep in the backseat with her head on her Harvard book bag.

Riley leans his head back against the car seat and closes his eyes and sighs slightly. Even his eyelashes are red. A bunch of older kids at school call him "Mr. Red," which I think is absolutely, completely cool.

Chapter Two

When I walk into my apartment, I see my mom at the end of the hall in the little kitchen. She's wearing a black-and-white plaid outfit. There's an umbrella at the bottom of her closet that matches it. My mom either looks like a *Vogue* magazine ad or a chessboard—I'm not sure which. But I know she's going out because she's tapping her keys on the kitchen counter.

I'm late and she's anxious to leave. Maybe she's planning to go to Filene's Basement or maybe not. Maybe she's going someplace altogether different. I really don't know. She's wearing shiny, slippery nylons, and she slides her feet in and out of her two soft white boats for shoes.

My mom brushes past me now going out the door. I follow her, and by the time I catch up, she's already in the wrought-iron cage elevator, wire-mesh door shut, pulled across her face. I'm standing in the hallway. She's talking to me as the elevator goes down the shaft into the workings of the building, past four floors to the foyer.

"I hope you're not running around with that Desmona and her brother anymore. Those rich kids do all sorts of crazy things because they're starved for attention," she calls up the shaft. "Can't you see that?"

Suddenly I bolt down the tiny back stairs. They twist around narrow and tight, but I make it to the first floor before my mom. I'm already there when she opens the wire-mesh door and steps out. I grew up in this foyer. I used to play hopscotch on the marble tiles here. One time, I fell asleep on these steps. It wasn't until Mr. Krimms came home from teaching and stepped over me that I woke up. I knew it was him when I saw the ragged-looking, roughed-up briefcase and the sheets of music sticking out of the top, the first bars of Moonlight Sonata looking me in the face.

I used to sit on these steps a lot when no one was home upstairs, when my dad was in the basement or the attic fixing broken things—pipes, wires, furnace valves. I used to sit out here and play *Rilly, rally, ree, I see something you don't see* by myself, taking both sides, being me and someone else, looking for something red or green, pretending I didn't already know what it was.

I sit on these steps again now, as if they are my spot, my "psychic spot," like I read in *Woman's Day* magazine. "It's the spot in your house where you find yourself drawn, where you're the most comfortable. It's your *psychic spot.*"

My mom is going out the door. She has a red patent-leather purse over her shoulder. *Rilly, rally, ree, I see something you don't see, and the color is red.* She's in a nervous flurry—hurrying somewhere. She's like a boat leaving the shore, and I must be the dock, sitting here on these steps, never moving, never going anywhere.

I follow my mom out onto Brattle Street. Students pour by us going the opposite direction as if we're swimming against the current—Harvard boys, Radcliffe girls, everybody with green book bags.

I want to tell my mom about a dream I had. I get out about a line before I realize how dumb it is. It was a dumb dream.

"I dreamed my room was yellow," I say to her.

"Ah," says my mom. She's big on psychological interpretation—like reading into everything. She took a psychology class last year at night, and ever since then, she's been analyzing everything. Like she probably thinks yellow means something—like loneliness, like yellow means lonely. *Rilly, rally, ree, I see something you don't see, and the color is yellow.* Yellow is the room I wish I had—a yellow bed, yellow walls, everything warm like sunshine.

I can see my face reflected in my mom's red patent-leather purse. It's as shiny as a mirror. I can see my face, the long brown hair. I wish my hair were yellow, yellow like Christina Talbot's hair. She must be so perfect; her psychic spot must be everywhere.

At Sage's Grocery on the corner, my mom turns around and says, "Why don't you make grilled cheese sandwiches and tomato soup for your dad? I'll be back by ten. Okay, sweetie?"

We have soup a lot. Sometimes I'll even scorch the bottom of the pan, but my dad won't mind. He'll smile slightly—tilt his head, not say much. Or he'll tell me about one of his tenants in our building, like Mrs. Ethel Elgar—how she locked herself in her bathroom by mistake. So she turned on the water in the sink and let it overflow. "It was the only way to get my attention," my dad will tell me.

"Grilled cheese sandwiches are easy, aren't they, sweetie?" says my mom crossing the street, looking back the way a sailor looks back at the shore—a mixture of relief and sorrow, a tugging look.

Because of those black-and-white checks, I can see my mom way down the street taking the curve into Harvard Square. If I were in an airplane, I could see her from miles up. I could see that pattern. If I were lost in a sea of people, she would be easy to find, wouldn't she?

I go into a cafeteria two doors up and order a raspberry lime rickey. I take it back to the last dark table in the place. In the middle of the room, at center tables, Harvard professors are laughing and arguing. They are talking about constellations and star formations and unimaginable distances of which I have no comprehension. Mr. Krimms shows me maps of the night sky, but a lot of the time I'm just whistling and hardly listening. I sit back in the corner sipping my drink. The lime is bitter and the raspberry sweet.

If I ran out now and climbed a tower, went to the top of the Harvard Coop or climbed up to the roof of our apartment building, could I still see my mother in her chessboard dress, working her way through the crowd? Deep down in this dark wooden booth drinking my raspberry lime rickey, I remember what I saw in Copley Square. It pours over me like ice water, and then I forget it again.

I have been playing the piano for about eight years. I had my first piano performance with Mr. Krimms when I was twelve. I remember the first piece I played. It was called "The Butterfly Rumba."

Before my performance, Mr. Krimms and I had rearranged his apartment. We tried to make it look like a little auditorium, moving his couches around and pushing his little fish tank sideways so you could still see the flat striped fish in there making bubbles. Then we baked cookies shaped like musical notes, and we set them out around the room.

My mom and dad and Mrs. Ethel Elgar rode down from the apartments above in the wrought-iron elevator. My dad was wearing a chrysanthemum in his lapel, and Mrs. Ethel Elgar had a bouquet of forsythias for the piano. My mom had her purse with her, bright and shiny — ready to go. Such a bright red color, every time I turned around I could see it out of the corner of my eye.

Mr. Krimms waited in front of the tiny audience. He was standing still, but he was full of movement, like a candle flickering. He looked out at the group and smiled. "This afternoon I would like to introduce my piano student," he said.

Mr. Krimms knew things about me. He knew I didn't have any friends at school. I'm not sure, but I thought, at the time, he knew about Copley Square and what I'd seen there that day, even though I've never told anyone. Ever. "This student has been playing the piano since she was five years old. As soon as I began to teach her, she advanced very rapidly. As you can imagine, I am very pleased," he said, and he began to beam at the audience, his whole body shining through his worn tweed suit, his head tilted shyly. "Now I should like very much to introduce to you my student, Rachel Townsend." The little audience clapped, but there were so few of them, they sounded to me more like shorebirds making a small ruckus.

I played slowly and carefully. Mr. Krimms nodded his head up and down with the music, the notes fluttering like butterfly wings, or at least they were supposed to. "Hesitant," Mr. Krimms whispered. "Hesitant like a butterfly landing, Rachel, and then up and off, up and off."

I was wearing patent-leather shoes. They were ever-so-slightly tight. My dad sat in the corner. My mom was on the couch. I wanted them to be sitting together. As I played, I remembered. I remembered coming out of the subway in Copley Square, the sound of the train roaring. The day everything changed. I tried to keep it away, but it came with the notes—hesitant, hesitant. When I was done with the piece, I heard the four of them clapping. They went on and on. I stood up, dizzy, as if motion sick from the subway. I leaned forward, bowed at the waist, and fainted.

## Chapter Three

Desmona lies on the flat, hot rock at Walden Pond, her clothes dripping a dotted line around her body that reminds me of a paper-doll outline. Riley's flopped out nearby, his head on Desmona's arm, almost like Raggedy Andy leaning against his dark-haired Raggedy Ann. They are lying there as if they have no bones and no joints.

"So, where does your mother go?" Desmona asks me, looking at the sea-green pond. Water skaters and gnats jet across the surface. Below them, puffing white clouds and distorted hills flicker and then divide into waves and disappear.

"I don't know where she goes," I say. "She just

puts on a dark hat and sunglasses, and walks to Harvard Square and slips down into the subway."

"Do you think she's a CIA agent?" says Woolsey, throwing a small stone into the pond, which has suddenly gone dark, almost black, as the sun goes behind a cloud.

Woolsey has been sitting at the edge of Walden Pond with his legs in the water up to his knees. That's as far as he'll go. He's never gone all the way in. He can't swim. In fact, he hasn't been out of Cambridge much before. "I guess I'm kind of a city slicker," he says.

"And not all that slick," says Riley, poking him with his foot and smiling.

"Nah, I guess not too slick either." Woolsey throws another pebble, and it scatters the clouds and hills and trees into a million rippling pieces.

"Come on, Rachel. Don't dwell on it. Maybe she's just going shopping," says Desmona.

We come out here a lot, partly because it's peaceful and partly because this is where Desmona's mother died. She drowned out here. She fell out of a boat. She was a poet. Someone had made a record of her reading her poems. On the record cover it said, *Jean McKarroll Reads,* and there was a

1950s woman sitting at a table, looking down as if she were about to begin playing the piano.

Desmona and Riley and Woolsey and me, and sometimes Mickey and Darcy, come out here every week because Desmona wants to and because Riley does just about anything Desmona wants. Not that he doesn't have a lot of other friends. He does. In fact, half the time he's off and away, and we don't even know where he is. But he and Des hang around together a lot. They're just like a pair of salt- and pepper shakers. (Des is the pepper.)

I don't know how it is we got to talking about my mother and how she seems to weave through the crowds in Harvard Square. And then she's gone. And I don't know where she's going. Maybe it's our mothers, the thread that winds between me and Desmona.

"Aren't we picketing the lunchroom tomorrow, Desmona?" I ask, trying to change the subject. "Aren't they serving veal Parmesan again?" Every Wednesday they serve veal Parmesan at Cambridge High and Latin, and every Wednesday we picket. We sing, we cry, we beg, but they keep on serving up those baby calves.

"Oh, you're right," says Desmona. "I forgot. Are the posters still at your apartment, Woolsey?"

"You bet," says Woolsey.

"Oh, I love you, Alfred Pontiac," says Desmona, getting up and hugging Woolsey. "I love you, Alfred Pontiac the third."

Desmona hugs everybody a lot and says she loves them, but she doesn't mean "love, love."

As far as "love, love" goes, I don't have much firsthand knowledge. I've been on one date so far, with the boy who sits behind me in U.S. history class. He asked me to go to the movies, and we went to see *Lawrence of Arabia* in Harvard Square. Afterward, at Schrafft's Ice Cream Parlor, he told me his father was a spy. He said it with a very plain, forward face. I knew by the way he said it that he'd been needing to tell someone for a long time.

As for Desmona, she says she "love, loves" Mr. Burns, our English teacher, which doesn't surprise me since he reads poetry to the class and Des is a poetry nut like Riley. She's always reading Henry Wadsworth Longfellow. She sits at her desk in the front of the class and doesn't move for the whole forty-five minutes. Burns *is* spellbinding, with his careless blond hair and black-rimmed glasses. He delivers the poems with an almost English accent and with the "lilt" I'm looking for in my piano playing ("Lilt, Rachel, more lilt"). He read us *Julius Caesar* last fall, and it's still lilting in my ears. "O! pardon me, thou bleeding piece of earth, / That I am meek and gentle with these butchers; / Thou art the ruins of the noblest man / That ever lived in the tide of times. / Woe to the hand that shed this costly blood!"

Riley takes a running leap now and soars into the air, then dives into Walden Pond. I can tell he's taken diving lessons at Cambridge High and Latin. His pitch is absolutely perfect. Both he and Desmona have refused to go to prep school, though their stepmother is constantly pushing them to. "Why should we go to a better school than you or anyone else?" says Desmona. "Is that fair?"

Riley turns over and floats on his back. His red curls are falling below into the wet darkness. He's reciting a poem. I hear lines now and then. The hot spring sun stills the surface of the pond, rocking Riley's body softly in the water. The spring heat makes all things melt into greenness—the air, the ground, the trees still as death.

Riley climbs up out of the water like a great vision, like a ghost rising up from the dark center of

Walden Pond. Some people think it's strange that Riley and Desmona swim in the pond where their mother died. I don't think it's strange at all. I think it's kind of sad.

The trees make a rustling sound now as the wind runs through them, and a wave of music washes through me. I can feel it. I can *almost* hear it, and then it slips away like water through my hands, leaving the trees singing with silence.

Riley throws a towel over his shoulder, and we all stand up with him and walk toward his little red car. Woolsey and I climb in the tiny backseat because we're both pretty little, and Desmona gets in the front. We drive out on the dirt road away from Walden Pond, back toward Cambridge.

Riley turns up the reel-to-reel tape machine, and that guy Bob Dylan yowls out his songs and sucks on a harmonica.

*The answer, my friend, is blowin' in the wind,*
*The answer is blowin' in the wind.*

Yes, we are blowing in the wind, all of us in Desmona's crowd—the forgotten ones, the ones who can't become the class president or make the cheerleading team or the soccer team or the football team. Yes, we're blowing in the wind, and all the way home the flowers along the highway bloom like crazy, even though it's just a big asphalt ugly world. They don't care. They just bloom anyway.

## Chapter Four

We have to stop at Woolsey's apartment to pick up the posters we made since they're serving veal at school tomorrow. There are diagrams with pictures of baby calves living their short, sad lives in these horrible little pens. They are not allowed to walk around in these little pens because the farmers want to fatten them up. They are fed huge amounts of grain, and they can't move.

"It's cruel beyond belief," Desmona will announce as people filter past, crowding into the lunchroom.

Woolsey will hand out little mimeographed flyers, and every time someone takes one, he will look at them and say, "Please."

"Do not eat this lunch," Desmona will call out.

I will hold up a sign that says, VEAL IS NOT A MEAL. IT'S MURDER.

Most of the kids will pass by unaware, uncaring. They'll stare at us for a second and then forget us. Some of the tough girls with foot-high teased hair and pointed black boots will call out as they walk by, "Gawd, you people are so sick."

"I just want them to take veal off the school menu," Desmona will say, trying to straighten her wrinkled shiny purple blouse. With Desmona, clothes glitter and shine, but they just don't hang right.

Mr. Red turns onto Storrow Drive now, and we sail by the Charles, where Harvard boys are whipping up and down the river in their crew boats. Sometimes they sing in unison, and we hear them. *I've got sixpence, jolly, jolly sixpence, I've got sixpence to last me all me life.*

Riley has his large freckled reddish hands gripped around the steering wheel. Then he lets go of one hand and throws his arm along the top of the seat and leans his head back, his red hair falling toward me. "So, where to, Woolsey?" he calls out.

"He lives in Rachel's building," says Desmona. Then she reaches in her book bag and pulls out a drawing she has made. She turns around and holds it up in front of her face. "It's just a rough sketch," she says. "It's of that sweet elephant I saw in the newspaper, the one that's so neglected. I want to do a big painting of her. And then I want to march through Harvard Square with it and beg people to stop mistreating animals."

"Oh, boy," says Woolsey. "With *your* painting? Bring out the mud pies."

"Quit it, Woolsey. I like my painting. I may not be Michelangelo, but Riley thinks I'm pretty good," says Des.

"Yeah, I think she puts a lot of interesting colors in her paintings," says Riley. "She's not afraid to use grays and browns. What *some* people call *mud*, others call *expressive*."

Desmona looks over at Woolsey and smiles.

"Hey, Riley," says Woolsey, "what about the time you ate the still life Desmona was painting while she was out of the room taking a break?"

"I didn't know she was painting those bananas," says Riley.

"Yeah," says Desmona, "when I got back to the canvas, there was no still life set up—just an empty plate. So I named the painting *The Vanishing*

*Point.* My teacher hated the painting, but he *loved* the title."

Riley pulls up in front of 87 Brattle Street, the U-shaped building full of part-time Radcliffe teachers, visiting scholars, elderly wives of dead professors, retired staff gardeners, and ancient secretaries to the office of the assistant dean. Actually, Woolsey and I are the only teenagers in the whole building. You'd think they'd replace this rickety old flying birdcage elevator, but they don't. In fact, that's just what it looks like to me, *a cage* just barely containing Desmona and Riley, who are both so tall. Riley's 6'2" and has to almost lean over, and Desmona is 5'10" and only thirteen years old. They are larger than everything around them.

Riley, in his tuxedo jacket, drying T-shirt, and wet khaki shorts, pulls the elevator door shut, and we ride up to Woolsey's. Woolsey looks kind of little standing there next to Riley, whose head is moving around, up and down. Riley twiddles his thumbs and whistles a few notes and then looks over at me and says, "Should I be nervous? Is this cage dangling by a thin ancient wire or anything like that?"

"It's okay," says Woolsey. "It only gets stuck

once in a while. Last time it happened, the ninety-two-year-old sisters from apartment 6C were in between floors for a couple of hours. They had just been to Sage's Grocery, so they were able to have a picnic lunch in here. It happens to them a lot, but they're used to it—they've lived in this building all their lives."

On the fourth floor, Riley pulls the gate back, bends at the waist, and says to me, *"Après vous, Madame."*

Woolsey moves out into the narrow hallway, goes to his door, and unlocks it. "My dad is too nervous to push his wheelchair over the crack between the floor and the elevator, so he doesn't get out much," says Woolsey, frowning and smiling at us at the same time. "Dad, I'm home," he calls out.

We go down a dark corridor past a crowded kitchen and into a larger living room with the curtains drawn across a length of windows and a Red Sox game on the radio blaring away. Woolsey's father is sitting in a wheelchair in the middle of the room, smoking a cigarette, listening to the Red Sox game. It's the eighth inning. The crowd is roaring, and the announcer has that revved-up crazy tone in his voice. Somebody just hit a home run. Woolsey's father slaps the arm of the wheelchair.

"By golly," he says, "they're winning. One of these days, Alfred, when I get back the use of my legs, I'm going to take you to a Red Sox game. We're gonna sit there on the third-base line near the dugout—the best seats in the house, Alfred."

"Dad," says Woolsey, "this is Desmona and Riley, and you know Rachel. They came to pick up those posters we made."

"Oh, yeah," says his father, "help yourself." He drags on his cigarette.

"May I open these curtains for you?" says Desmona. "I think it would be a lot cheerier with the sunlight." She goes over and pulls all the curtains away from the windows, lighting up the apartment with that high overcast Cambridge light, the Cambridge sky the color of a gray dove.

"Shut the curtains," says Sergeant Pontiac, putting his hands over his eyes. "Shut the curtains. Shut them." I lean over and pull the cord, and the curtains glide back across the long bank of windows, blocking out the late-afternoon sun.

Woolsey goes over to his dad and puts his hand on his arm. "Are we going to eat franks and fries at Fenway, Dad?" says Woolsey. "With ketchup?"

Sergeant Pontiac says, "I don't like the bright sun. Do you kids know about Omaha Beach?"

"Will you get ketchup or mustard on your franks, Dad?" Woolsey says.

And Sergeant Pontiac says, "Do you know where it is in Normandy, France?"

"Dad," says Woolsey.

"Have you ever heard of D-day? I was Sergeant Pontiac coming into Omaha Beach. We came in by water. Artillery everywhere. Guns, land mines, grenades—a sea of men climbing the sand dunes, shells going off every second."

"Dad," says Woolsey.

"I just kept thinking how that beach was going to look in ten years, with kids running in the water carrying these pails of sand. I just kept thinking of those mothers in the sunlight and those kids and those goddamned pails of sand. Those goddamned pails of sand. My buddies were dying all around me, and I didn't even know I'd been hit. All I thought about was those pails and that sunlight." Sergeant Pontiac is crying. I can see tears running down his cheeks.

Desmona goes over to him and puts her arm around his shoulder and says, "Sergeant Pontiac, do you know you have a wonderful son?"

Chapter Five

Riley throws the posters in the backseat of the car, and I hand Desmona a big sign with a photo of a sweet sad-eyed baby calf looking out at you with the word *murder* written under it. Desmona holds the sign up high as they drive off down the street, and I wave good-bye, watching that neat little red car buzzing away.

Not really wanting to go home yet, I cross the street and walk through the shady grounds toward a Radcliffe building. Downstairs, in the large main room of that building, there's a piano. It's cool and quiet in here, and the greenery outside the large window dances against the glass. I sneak in here often to practice and think. Sometimes I just sit at the piano with my hands on the keys, looking into its shiny black reflective surface, thinking of things, listening to Chopin in my head, wishing I could write a melody, a beautiful, simple melody of my own.

I'm just sitting here practicing some scales, watching the leaves in the trees tossing against the window, when Riley McKarroll walks in, in his tuxedo jacket, taking long Riley strides across the marble floor.

"There you are, Rachel. I thought you'd be here," he says, sitting down next to me. He plays a quick, jazzy blues piece. And then he puts his hands on the keys to stop the song, and a discordant, dead sound fills the room.

"Rachel, I want you to do me a flavor," says Riley.

"Chocolate or vanilla?" I say, smiling. Riley looks soft and mournful. His dark hazel eyes are wide open. I can see the greenery reflected in them, swaying in the wind.

"Rachel," he says, "I want you to call Christina for me. Desmona won't do it. She doesn't like Christina. Rachel, please."

"Call Christina?" I ask. "What do you want me

to say? I don't even know her. And how did you get back here so fast?"

"I parked at home and walked back. I was looking for you. Please?" he says again. Then he turns back to the piano and plays a longer jazzy sweet piece that melts me down to zero. Then negative zero . . . negative ten . . .

"Okay, sure, Riley. I'll do it. What shall I say?"

"I don't know," he says, still playing. "Tell her you're from the Hoover Vacuum Cleaner Company and you want to set up a good time to give the family a demonstration."

"Okay, Riley, but why?"

"Because I want to hear her voice. I *have* to hear her voice. She's got this beautiful voice."

We go over to a phone on the far wall and dial up the number that Riley has written on the crinkled corner of an envelope. I can tell by his hands that he's nervous.

The phone rings, and Riley has his head close to mine, leaning against the receiver trying to listen. It rings another buzz, and then a girl answers.

"Hello."

"Uh, hello, I'm calling from the, uh, Hoover Vacuum Cleaner Company. Uh, I was wondering if you . . . uh . . . ," and then I start laughing, and I can't stop.

"Who is this?" says the girl. "Is this Emily? Emily?"

I drop the phone and fall into the plastic couch in the lounge, laughing out of control.

Riley picks up the receiver, his face shining, his eyes toward the sky. He stands there listening for a minute. Then he hangs up the phone and throws himself into the couch next to me. He looks like he's been hit with something large and ringing. I'm still laughing and laughing. It just won't quit. Finally it does, and Riley and I just sit there in complete silence, neither one of us moving an inch.

All of a sudden, Riley jumps up and goes over to the piano and starts playing this fast jazz run. His fingers ripple like dominoes falling across the keys. His eyes are closed. His head is tipped back. The music rolls like water through the room. Listening to it, I feel like I have a birthday cake in my heart, all the candles burning, burning brightly.

*Chapter Six*

The lunchroom at Cambridge High and Latin is rather large . . . to put it mildly. The walls are prison gray, and the battery of windows along one side is covered in cagelike chain-link panels — to keep in or keep out, I'm not sure which. Already there is a multitude of students milling toward the cafeteria line. We are late getting set up because one of Desmona's sandals broke outside of biology class, Woolsey's combination wouldn't work on his locker, and I took the wrong corridor in the B building and ended up going down a long lopsided wooden hallway in the F wing, lost after being in this school for almost a year. That's how big this place is. Cambridge High and Latin is the oldest and largest high school in the country.

Desmona has just taped up the big picture of the soft-eyed, soft-eared baby calf across the walls outside the lunchroom. The rest of us take up our usual positions. I lean against the corner wall with my sign, which I conveniently hold over my face. I always do that. I stay in the background and follow along.

Darcy, who is also pretty shy, keeps putting her sign down and pulling up her socks. When Desmona first met her, Darcy had let her bangs grow down over her eyes, but now she holds them back with a rhinestone bobby pin that Desmona gave her. "It was my mother's," Des told Darcy. "Wear it in your hair. You will be beautiful, and for all I know, they could be real diamonds."

Woolsey is up near the double doors handing out flyers with a cheerful ready-to-go face. "Do not eat this lunch!" Desmona shouts. "Look at this beautiful baby calf."

In the sea of heads coming toward us, one of them stands out—taller, older, eyes narrowed, angry, moving closer.

"Oh, God," says Desmona. "It's Tuffy the Tugboat himself." (She means Mr. Tuffican, the principal of Cambridge High and Latin.) With him is a string of henchmen.

Jacob Birstin whistles from across the hall at Desmona, warning her. Several other kids from our group farther up the line whistle, fold up their signs, and walk into the lunchroom.

Mr. Tuffican emerges from the crowd like a warrior, like Mark Antony, Julius Caesar's greatest soldier. He backs Desmona and me and Darcy and Woolsey up against the wall. We are there with these warriors all around us, flat up against the poster of the calf (all that gentleness and those eyes).

Desmona says, "Tuffy the Tugboat, we want veal Parmesan taken off the menu."

All the woodwork in Mr. Tuffican's office is dark-stained natural wood. There's a plaster plaque on the wall above a door that says, *Omnia mutantur, nos et mutamur in illis, 1924*, which means, I think, thanks to Schwartz's Latin class, *All things change, and we change with them, 1924.*

Mr. Tuffican has gone into his inner chamber

with the door shut; he is preparing the three-day suspension papers for Desmona and me and Woolsey and Darcy.

Woolsey's sitting there kind of crying. He looks over at me and says, "I hope the social worker who visits us doesn't get wind of this."

Outside, Riley is pacing the hall, trying to get caught without a hall pass. He probably feels awful that he wasn't there. He was taking an exam in physics class and missed the whole thing. He's walking back and forth, back and forth out there. Riley is so tall that the basketball coach here is always trying to get him to join the team again, but he won't. "Why should I spend all my time tossing a peach into a peach basket?" he says. "That's about all it is."

We can hear someone walking up the hall in high heels. They click closer, louder, and clearer, and then Gretchen appears with her blond hair in a French twist and her Grace Kelly little white gloves. She has gray eyes that skim over me and Woolsey and land on Desmona. She sits down next to her and says, "So what have you done now, Desmona? And with your father being such an important man. How could you do this to him? This is absurd. You belong in boarding school. You should be studying and learning to be a young lady."

"I don't have to *learn* to be a young lady," says Desmona. "I *am* a young lady. And I'm not going to prep school. Ever."

Desmona looks down at her hands.

"You know what you remind me of? In my country during the war which was so terrible, there were two children, fifteen and sixteen years old, a brother and a sister with an underground organization they started. It was called the White Rose. My mother knew of them. These two children were very daring. They tried to work against Hitler, which of course was very noble and very brave.

"Do you know what happened to them?" Gretchen asks, staring at us, Woolsey with his hands over his eyes and Darcy looking gray and thin in her hand-me-down plaid dress. "Do you know what happened to them? They were both shot and killed. Fifteen and sixteen years old. Boom, all gone. No more brother and sister."

Mr. Tuffican comes out of his office and hands each of us the suspension papers. Then he pauses and decides to let Darcy go with just a warning since she's never been in his office before.

Darcy gets up and slides out the door, turning

47

back toward us with a mournful look. Then she moves slowly down the hall like a little moon all alone in the sky.

Woolsey is sniffling and wiping his nose. Gretchen says, "I'm sorry about all this, Mr. Tuffican. I will call you." She leads Desmona out into the hall; their voices echo down the wide flight of wooden stairs. They pass Riley out there, leaning against someone's locker—leaning over like he's trying to catch his breath.

Woolsey and I go out the front doors after Desmona, out into the bright sun and strange quiet that hangs in the air when you leave school early. We pass the black Mercedes parked at the curb. Gretchen and Desmona don't look our way, and they don't offer us a ride back to Harvard Square.

## Chapter Seven

Being suspended for me will mean that I'll have to do all sorts of fetching and carrying around the apartment building, my father being the janitor and superintendent of 87 Brattle Street. Superintendent, janitor, custodial engineer, "A rose by any other name would smell as sweet," as Mr. Burns my English teacher would say, or "A rose is a rose is a rose." And a janitor is a janitor, and he's my father. He takes care of our whole building, and in my spare time I have to help.

These next three days, I'll probably have to haul the trash down the tiny back stairs for the ninety-two-year-old Butterfield sisters in apartment 6C.

Or you might find me mopping up a bathroom floor in apartment 3B because the toilet over-flowed. I'm not exactly looking forward to it.

Woolsey is harping on the social worker stuff and how she's been talking about moving him to foster care. "I love my dad," he says to me as we head along the shady street toward Harvard Yard. "I want to live with him even if he is a little stuck on D-day."

It's a beautiful day. Woolsey and I are walking in the guilty, silent landscape of an early afternoon dismissal. We're the only students out here except for some Rindge toughs on the corner—they never go to class; they never go home; they never eat or go to sleep. They're always on that corner—the same five guys in black leather jackets.

As we walk along, I'm thinking about Riley slouching against the lockers, looking tall and tur-bulent when we passed him. Sometimes I just kind of want to say his name out loud—*Riley McKarroll Riley McKarroll Riley McKarroll*—but I never do. That boy from my U.S. history class asked me out again recently, but I didn't want to go. Why? Be-cause he isn't *the one*. "Who is *the one?*" Desmona is always asking me, and I say, "Oh, never mind, Desmona. Never mind."

Woolsey is leaping over the cracks in the sidewalk, expending all this extra energy as usual. Most of the time he wears penny loafers for shoes and keeps two real Indian head pennies in both the little slots on the top, but then he's always worrying someone will steal his shoes, even while he's wearing them. But that's Woolsey for you.

We cross the street, and after a while we walk through Harvard Yard, some of the flowering trees gently dropping their petals on the ground as we pass them. It's quiet in here, too, until we walk through the brick-and-iron gate and into Harvard Square. Then the silence is gone. This is the center of the world. Here you can buy a newspaper in any language you want and oranges and apples that are so huge they look more like melons. There is a guy with a camera who for two dollars can hand you a photo of yourself in three minutes. It develops in his hands while he counts. Woolsey and I had one taken once, but I hated the way I looked, so I ripped my face in half. Woolsey grabbed the pieces and stuffed them in his algebra book, and he wouldn't give them back to me no matter how much I begged.

I usually love to walk everywhere around here, even in the winter. I never take the subway. Woolsey loves the subway. He calls it the MTA and knows the whole system by heart, all the stops in the Boston area. He loves to sing the song about the guy named Charlie who never got off the subway because they raised the rates while he was onboard and he didn't have enough money with him to get off. I only rode the subway once by myself, to Copley Square that day. *Clickety-clack. Clickety-clack,* all by myself through the roaring dark tunnels.

"What are you going to tell your mother?" says Woolsey now, his eyes rolling up at me.

"We'll see," I say, stopping on the other side of the Square in front of a clothing store called Dresses and Dreams & Co., where my mother works. "I'll be back in a minute. The manager doesn't like it when more than one of us comes in at a time."

I leave Woolsey sitting outside on a bench, and I push through the glass doors at Dresses and Dreams. I pass a row of lonely-looking mannequins all dressed up in suits and scarves and hats, and right away I start looking for my mom. There are so many dressing rooms and corners and nooks, she could be anywhere.

Someone comes out of a front dressing room carrying a huge load of dresses. I can't see who it is underneath that pile, but I'm guessing it's my mom. I can tell by the shoes—white pumps.

"Mom," I call out, and then the person puts down the pile of dresses on a nearby table and I look over. It's not my mom's face or hair or anything. It's not my mom at all. It's Nan Southwick.

I hurry away back by the rows of slacks, so many of them, thousands of pairs, armies of slacks and skirts. Who will wear them all? Who will they be? Where will they go? "Mom?" I call out.

Now Nan Southwick is standing outside a dressing room. She's calling in, "So how is it? Does it fit?"

A woman behind the curtained-off area says, "I need something really special, something really unusual, not ordinary." She pushes the curtain aside, and I see she's a pretty woman with blond hair. She has a hunched enlarged shoulder and a slight limp. She looks in the mirror at herself, fluffs her light, wispy hair. Nan Southwick ties the bow on the blouse under the woman's chin.

"This is all silk," says Nan, "with French buttons."

The woman looks at herself in the mirror again, and then a slight frown streaks across her expression. "No. No. I need something really wonderful," she says.

I move to the back of the store, passing a lady in a red dress standing in front of a three-way mirror. The lady turns around and around. "Mom," I call out again.

I walk down an aisle of silk dresses. I let my hand drag along, feeling the silk against my palm. When I was younger, while my mom was working, I used to throw myself into racks of dresses like this. I would be on the floor, in the dark silk world under the racks behind the clothes, watching people's feet go by, waiting for my mom to be done—to be all done, to be ready to go home.

The manager comes out of the back. He's in a big hurry. He's always in a big hurry. "Which section is my mother, Mary Townsend, working in today?" I ask him. He blows by me with an aqua evening gown sailing in his arms.

"Mary T isn't working today." He calls her Mary T because there's another Mary working here, too. Mary T sounds so strange, as if it's not my mother at all, but someone else altogether.

"Yes, she is," I say. "Maybe you didn't notice. She left the house this morning dressed for work. She told me. Didn't you see her? She was wearing a rose-colored dress and white pumps—

like *those* shoes," I say, pointing to Nan South-wick's feet.

"No, Rachel, she wasn't scheduled for today. She's working tomorrow," says the manager, swinging his arm around. The aqua dress follows, lifting and fluttering — a bird ready to fly, a boat in the harbor.

"That can't be. There's been a mistake. You're wrong," I say, and I start for the door. The walls and doors are all glass. My mother tells me sometimes she finds a bird lying on the ground when she comes into work in the morning — a bird that mistook the glass for sky.

When I get outside, Woolsey is still sitting on one of the cement benches set up along the street. He's so short his feet swing, not quite touching the ground. He's pretty sure he'll grow soon. He measures himself every day. "I haven't hit my growing spurt yet," he says, looking at me with a little cloud on his face.

We cross the street, passing Radcliffe girls in leather sandals like Des wears. Motor scooters roar by, and just turning the corner is an old woman with a feather in her hat and a big white parrot perched on her shoulder. As we walk into Sage's,

Woolsey says, "What did your mom say about getting suspended?"

"I don't know," I answer, and Woolsey lets it go—a kite with a loosened string floating off into the sky.

# Chapter Eight

As soon as we get to 87 Brattle, Woolsey hurries into the elevator and rides up to his floor, looking at me like a guilty prisoner through the bars as he rides up. I stand hesitant, hesitant outside of Mr. Krimms's door. Why am I here? It is not Friday, the day I take piano lessons. I can hear music coming through the door. It draws me in like a river.

Mr. Krimms seems to know things about me even when I don't tell him anything. I used to come here when I couldn't find my dad, when he was somewhere in the depths of the building, but I didn't know where. Mr. Krimms used to let me leap off the back of his couch trying to fly. He didn't care about the springs. When I first took an interest in the piano, he let me pound on the keys whenever I wanted. Slowly he began to show me how to read notes, how to lilt and lean, how to swim with the music.

I knock on Mr. Krimms's door, apartment 1A. Mr. Krimms is in his brown velvet bathrobe, and he's holding a hot cup of tea when he comes to the door. He steps over piles of unopened mail and folded unread newspapers on the floor.

"Oh, Rachel, come in," he says. "It looks like I have a touch of the flu. I'm glad for your company; come in."

Mr. Krimms loves the night sky and has large blue maps on his walls with white dots all over them that represent constellations like the Great Bear and the Big Dipper. He also has his own names for some of the star formations. There's a comet he calls the "Madman's Hair" and he's always talking about the constellation of the "Mending Heart."

When I go into Mr. Krimms's apartment, it feels as if I'm walking into a planetarium. It has the same peculiar darkness, the same weird fabrication of outer space. Some of Mr. Krimms's maps of the sky light up with fluorescent white ink when he turns off all the lights, so his walls are full of shining stars.

He also has an indigo-blue globe that sits on his coffee table. It's larger than the usual globes you see, and the blue has something special about it—a kind of strange iridescence.

I step over the unopened mail and put my green book bag, which is just like Desmona's, on a chair. Then I throw myself onto Mr. Krimms's couch, and every inch of me uncurls and rests, the way it feels when you're finally home. In front of me on the coffee table is the blue globe. I lean over it as if I am falling toward it or being pulled by gravity.

"How did school go? It was a half day?" Mr. Krimms asks.

"Not exactly," I say, and then I reach forward and give the globe a spin. "Where did you get this globe, Mr. Krimms?" I ask.

Mr. Krimms looks over at me and smiles, and doesn't answer because he knows I am just changing the subject. Still, he never will tell me where he got the globe.

"Not exactly?" he says.

"I stopped in to see my mom at work today, but she was on her lunch break," I say, giving the globe another spin because whenever I do, I always get this sense of possibility. I could go anywhere I want someday—to England, France, Italy. I always feel better with the blue globe spinning in my hands, as if anything were possible.

Usually when I spin it and stop somewhere, my finger on a country, I'll say, "Mr. Krimms, have you been here?"

And he will say, "Oh, yes. I was there a long time ago. It's a wonderful country," and he'll tell me all about it, what it looks like and what it feels like to be there.

Then usually I play the Chopin piece I've been practicing on Mr. Krimms's little spinet piano. And Mr. Krimms keeps his eyes closed, and then when something seems wrong—too fast or too uneven—he'll say, "Oh, more lilt, Rachel. This is the part that must lilt and lilt and lilt."

I don't get to take piano lessons from Mr. Krimms for free. It's kind of an exchange. I take care of things in the apartment in the summer for him when he's gone. I feed his fish and water his huge collection of potted amaryllis lilies. He has over twenty-five different varieties. Only one of them hasn't bloomed yet.

"My mom was on her lunch break. That's what

the manager told me," I say, and then I slip back farther into Mr. Krimms's couch. I let my hair fall over my face like a veil, and I look down through it to the floor.

"Ah," says Mr. Krimms. "I see. You know, Rachel, sometimes when something's bothering someone, they can make a kind of cocoon like a little wall around themselves. You know, that isn't always such a good idea. Sometimes it is better to talk about things."

Does Mr. Krimms know about what I saw in Copley Square? Is he talking about that shadow on my wall at night, shivering and flickering?

"Well," he says, "shall we put on Pablo Casals playing his beautiful cello—Nocturne in E-flat by Chopin? I just bought the record at the Coop last week, and I can't stop listening to it—it's so lovely." And he walks over to his record shelf and pulls a flat black record out of its sleeve and puts it on the record player, and the room fills up with beautiful trembling music. Around and around the record turns, just like Mr. Krimms's blue globe, spinning, spinning in my hands.

# Chapter Nine

*I* didn't stay as long as I usually do at Mr. Krimms's apartment because he said he wasn't feeling well. We're so excited about one of his amaryllis lilies. The one that never bloomed before has a big bud on it now. We have been feeding and watching and fussing over this lily, waiting and hoping all winter, wondering what it will look like when it finally blooms. It's the one called the butterfly lily. The whole time I was at his apartment, Mr. Krimms just kept walking around the lily and saying, "Oh my, my, what have we here, Rachel?"

When I get upstairs to our apartment, no one is home, of course. I push the door open (we never lock it) and go down the hall into my room. I turn on the light and put my book bag down. Two of my cats, Wadsworth and Julius, come up and sit beside me.

I pick up Julius and hold him on my shoulder. I just keep thinking that I didn't check all the changing rooms at Dresses and Dreams & Co. I forgot a whole string of them in the back, the ones the employees use. I should have looked for my mom in there. Why didn't I?

I open my book bag and pull out my notebooks. Sheet music scatters to the floor. Other people's music. Not mine. Not anymore. Probably never again.

I try to do a little homework, but I can't concentrate, so I start writing Riley's name all over a page of my notebook—*Riley Red* and then *Riley and Rachel 4 ever.* The apartment is dark beyond my room. My room is a little lighted cave in a dark woods. What if I called Riley up right now and told him how I feel about him? What would he do? What if I ran over there and stood in the hydrangea bushes like a crazy Juliet and called out, "Riley, I'm here. I love, love you. I can't live, live without you."

It's cold in here. I wonder where my dad is. Funny thing about this apartment building—even with all these people living here, it's still easy to get lonely.

I'm just writing out *Riley, Riley, Riley* when the phone rings. Yes, I have an extension in my room. I got it for my thirteenth birthday. It was from my mom. There was a card with it that said, "Happy thirteenth. Every teen should have one of these!" I also have a princess canopy bed, which my parents gave me for Christmas another year.

My phone is still ringing. I let it go a few times before I answer it because I don't want to seem like an eager beaver. I'm guessing it's Des. I lie back and pick up—putting the receiver to the window glass, where a pigeon sits on the ledge cooing.

"What was that?" says Desmona.

"My cousin from Nebraska is here visiting. She can't talk. All she can do is coo," I say.

"Ho, ho, ho, very funny," says Des. "Listen to this . . . Daddy didn't get in last night. We got a telegram. He'll be another three weeks. And I was all dressed and ready to go. Gretchen and I had a huge fight about my outfit. You know, my complete new orange ensemble with sequins sewn all over it. It took me hours to sew on all those sequins, and you saw the turban. Gretchen *hated* the turban, so we had this big showdown. I was crying and Gretchen was crying and then the doorbell rings and it's a telegram—three more weeks till Daddy comes home."

"Well, as Burns would say, 'Life goes on, Miss McKarroll.'" Burns calls everyone by their surnames: Miss Townsend, Miss McKarroll, Mr. Pontiac.

"Speaking of Burns," she says, "I won't be seeing him for three whole days. But I'll write him a poem. I'll bring it in and leave it on his desk, unsigned. He'll find it and wonder who wrote this great sensitive love poem. He'll be all baffled and beautiful when I come back. Oh, Rachel, I have to get out of here. I can't be with Gretchen for three days straight. I'll go insane."

"You already are, Desmona," I say.

"No, really, you don't understand. She's locked me in my room. I can't go anywhere. A few hours ago, she shoved an application to Deerfield Academy under my door. I'm thinking of calling the police," says Des. "Or better yet, I'll plan an escape. Riley wants to go tomorrow to North Lockwell, Mass., on the ocean, because he thinks the Skylark is there."

"You mean Christina Talbot?" I say.

"As it so happens, that zoo is near there. Remember the picture I showed you—remember that sad elephant? Do you think we are capable of rescuing that elephant?"

"What do you mean, Des?" I say.

"Do you think Riley and me and you and Woolsey could actually pull something like that off? Do you think it's possible?"

"I don't know," I say. "How would we ever do it?"

"Well," says Des, "we'd have to get there first, but that's a cinch with Riley driving. I guess the hard part would be getting the elephant out of there."

"Yeah, how would you move a ten-ton elephant, Desmona? Forget it; you're crazy."

"No, no, no, it's so simple. Of course! That's it. You *walk* the elephant out. You don't move it by truck. You lead it on foot to safety *at night* when no one is around."

"Desmona, we're already suspended, and you are locked in your room. Just forget it."

"I'm cooking up a plan, Rachel. I'm not going to stay in this prison for three days. We'll have to run away. We'll have to work everything out carefully. Gretchen is watching me like a hawk. Remember that time we snuck out to get ice cream at midnight, and I got stuck up on the roof?" says Desmona. "Possible repeat performance. I will call you."

After I hang up the phone, I get off my bed and put Julius on the floor. Then I go down the narrow hall and out the door. I ride the elevator down, down into the basement. It's dark and smells of furnace oil. There is a little light coming from way back at the end of the long tunnel. A sooty glowing yellow light.

"Dad," I call out.

"Yoo-hoo," he calls back. And I wind my way down the tunnel under the workings of this great big building—sewer pipes, water pipes, electric lines, phone lines. It reminds me of a subway tun-nel—that dingy lightless light, the dark oily walls. It reminds me of the day I took the subway to Cop-ley Square. I had on my red sneakers. I sat hidden behind a Coke machine, waiting for the train in the big arched underground tunnel. I was watching my red sneakers. I was swinging my feet Woolsey-style, my face in the shadows. Not that many people waiting for the train—just me and an old smelly guy with his whole life in a bag on his lap and a couple of routine people down on the other end reading. Everything A-OK—waiting for the

Red Line into Boston and then switching to the Green Line. Me, I was in the shadows—got on a bright car when the doors drew open. Magic— open sesame—walked right in, flopped down on a seat, the dark window across from me reflecting my face, all the way to Copley Square my face and me in the flickering, changing darkness, riding along, *clickety-clack, clickety-clack.*

"Dad," I call out again.

And he says, "Yoo-hoo," again, and I move closer to the light at the end of the tunnel. I get there and stand in the doorway. My dad is lying on his back with a wrench in his greasy dark hands—the great reaching furnace above him, enormous, huge with many arms like one of those Indian gods Mr. Krimms is always showing me pictures of, like the great blue one with eight arms.

"Dad," I say, leaning against an old rusty pipe. "I got suspended from . . ."

"What's that, sweetie?" he says.

And then I change my mind. I decide not to say anything at all. It's better this way. It's better he doesn't know anything. My dad is pretty hysterical about me not going to school, since he dropped out himself when he was sixteen to play the saxophone. He started a jazz band called the Hot

Weather Horns, and he played all over Pittsburgh, Pennsylvania, for a couple of years till he got so broke, he had to take a regular job.

"Dad," I say again. I look over at him. My dad is small in the tiny circle of light and helpless-looking, really, under the giant furnace and the giant building above. As I look over at him, he almost reminds me of a child in a small cradle of light, in a great dark world.

# Chapter Ten

At 4 A.M. the phone rings once. I'm sleeping all wrapped up like a mummy, tight as a cocoon in my blankets. The phone is right by my head, so I grab it quick. I go, "Hello?"

And the voice goes, "Hi!" It's a real daytime voice, and it belongs to my crazy friend Desmona. "I *have* to get out of here. I'm a real prisoner. I'm not kidding you, Rachel. I am locked in. You and Woolsey have to come over *now*."

"Desmona, it's four in the morning. There's nothing out there but lurking cats and criminals."

"Rachel, it has to be now while the big G is asleep." Des calls her stepmother that a lot. "Come on, Rachel, we have to leave from here."

"Leave?" I say.

"Yes," says Des. "We are going to try to save that elephant, Rachel. Riley thinks it's a great idea. Christina's summerhouse is in the next town over. He thinks she might be there. Just wake up Woolsey and come over right now."

⌖

I slip down the long hall past the living room. My father is asleep on the couch, his arms flung out like he's doing a back float. Wadsworth is crossing the room, going in and out of the shadows on the floor, looking at me with his big shining eyes.

My mother is sleeping in the bedroom. The door is shut. I can't see her sleeping, but she must be in there. She has to be. Then I see her soft white pumps like two boats docked near the sofa. Her shoes are here. My mother's shoes. My father's shoes are here, too, tossed around the room, the gangly stretching laces, the isolated bodies turned over, facing into the rug.

I stop for a minute and try to remember when the three of us went somewhere together. Did we ever? My father always had to be here on call, couldn't leave, like an anchor, and yet I could never find him. So many places he could be. The curtains are drawn and breathe like white ghosts at the window.

I tiptoe over to the table where all things pile up—newspapers, letters. My father's keys lie there on their fat shiny ring, the keys to everything in the world just lying there in the light from the street lamps outside. My dad stirs, turns over. His arm falls to the floor like it's weighted and sinking deeper and deeper into the rug. I slip the key to Woolsey's off the ring.

I step out into the hall, shutting Wadsworth in. I ride the old elevator down to Woolsey's floor, looking out through the bars as I go down, at the dark unknown spaces in between the floors. I get to Woolsey's door, and then I take my father's key and turn the lock.

I go straight to Woolsey's room, and I stand in the doorway, the light falling behind me. "Woolsey, wake up," I whisper, remembering there was one time my mother and I went out together. My dad stayed home. He couldn't leave the building unattended. We went to see a movie. There were subtitles. I was too young to understand all of it. It was about a little girl who had been blind, and then in the end, her sight was restored. And it was snowing, and the little girl held out her hands and said, "So this is snow. So this is snow. How beautiful the snow."

"Woolsey," I say again. "Wake up."

Woolsey sits up. He looks like a baby in his soft cowboy PJs. He rubs his eyes. He looks at me acceptingly, almost like I'm the ghost of his mother or something. "Okay," he says softly. "Sure. Okay."

✑

We get out of Woolsey's pretty easily. His dad takes sleeping pills, and once he's asleep, he's practically dead. We slide out the main door downstairs and go into the cold night air, darting down Brattle Street and crossing into the gardens at the Henry Wadsworth Longfellow house. There are soft spotlights on the huge yellow house and lawn. We cross under the enormous flowering cherry tree and cut through the spotlights, mosquitoes whining in the dark spaces.

We come out on Desmona's side lawn through a thick hedge of azalea bushes, and then we're in front of her house. Even at night, looking up at it, it could be the White House in Washington or something. Riley and his friend Mickey are always making jokes about holding press conferences on the front lawn. Desmona says the house belonged to an English admiral during the Revolution. "This house was a Tory stronghold," Desmona once said, flinging a book across the room. "Isn't that disgusting?"

Then her stepmother floated by and said, "Now, now, Desmona. Don't do such things. From where do you learn to throw books?"

I look up now to the second floor and see that Desmona's window is open wide. There's a length of rope hanging out of it. Woolsey and I stand there in the shadows, waiting and looking up. Then Desmona leans out the window. She's holding up a plaster mask. She growls behind it in a whispering, quiet way.

"Desmona, what are you doing? What the heck is that?" says Woolsey.

"This is the death mask of e. e. cummings. He was a famous poet. Riley took me to this sculptor's house. There was a whole pile of these masks. They were seconds. The sculptor was about to destroy them and only keep the good one. There's only supposed to be one in the whole world. But *I* have the other one. I put it under my jacket and brought it home. Isn't it neat?" Desmona whispers, taking the mask off and putting it in her book bag. Then she wraps herself around the rope and kind of throws herself out the window, saying, "Here goes nothing." She slides down the side of the house, knocking against the shutters, having a laughing fit all the way.

Woolsey says, "Desmona, quit it. Your step-mother's going to wake up." Desmona lands in the middle of a mock orange bush, flowers and darkness all around her. She's still laughing like a maniac, lying there among stars of white petals. Then she reaches in her book bag and gets out the mask again and puts it on and growls at Woolsey.

"Grrrr," she goes.

"Shut up," says Woolsey.

"Come on, you guys," I say. "Let's get out of here." We pull Des to her laughing feet. She's heavy, wearing a bunch of extra clothes like a runaway. When we pull her up, she's still laughing, but in the moonlight, I can see that the purple eye shadow under her eyes is streaked and smeared as if she was crying earlier.

At the edge of the yard, we pause, and Desmona tosses the death mask of e. e. cummings under a forsythia bush. As we sneak off into the darkness of Brattle Street, it lies there under the night flowers gently smiling.

We're like three ghosts in the cold blue Harvard Yard—sitting on the steps of the Fogg Art Museum, waiting for Riley to pick us up in an hour or so. From where we are, we can look in and see the Joan of Arc painting striped with shadows. Even so, Joan of Arc's face seems to be lit up from within. "I couldn't leave town without seeing it one more time," says Desmona, looking off toward something far away.

Soon we move on like a grazing herd to new ground. We go back to the Square and sit on the curb outside a shoe store. I remember being in that shoe store when I was younger. My mother was buying me a pair of shoes, patent-leather ones for my piano performance. I had one shoe on and one shoe off, sitting there like a hospital patient. My dad was supposed to stop by and see what we'd picked out. But he didn't show up. We waited almost an hour.

Then my mom got mad and called him. He wasn't there, probably with a tenant, maybe in the basement. We bought the shoes in a huff, all upset, all mixed-up. I forgot to tell my mom the shoes were too tight. They pinched my toes to death.

We walk along the streets, wandering a little now, the whole world looking to me like a blue Picasso painting. Desmona stops in front of a small art gallery. She stands there looking in.

"Look at those landscapes. God, I could never do that. They're *so* good," she says. Desmona's room at home is full of her paintings. Most of them are of sad women painted in muddy dark purples and browns. Her art teacher, Mr. Clyde, tells her she has absolutely no ability, but that does not deter my friend Desmona.

"Can you imagine how good it would feel to paint a landscape like that?" says Desmona, resting her head against the window glass, closing her eyes.

Woolsey leans over toward me and quietly says, "Do you know what Desmona's planning?" Then he looks around, stretches his arms up, and says, "You know, I think this suspension business has a medicinal effect on me. I feel like I'm going to grow three inches in my sleep tonight."

We're pretty sure no one will suspect I'm gone for a while. At home my door was shut. I put up a little note that said, *Sleeping late, headache.* My mom will go to work. My dad will snap up his gray coveralls and go off to attend to things, working his way through the building from the ground floor up. He won't even get near the fifth floor till dinnertime.

When I finally decided to tell my mother about the suspension last night, she walked away with her back to the room and wouldn't look at me. Then she said, "I blame those crazy rich kids you're hanging around with. They are like a pair of wild neglected ponies. The girl in particular. Her mother used to come in the store before she died mysteriously. Everything she bought had to be white—white flowers, white scarves. I heard she had a Christmas tree all year long, even in the summer. Her face is still clear in my mind. She had the biggest sad blue eyes."

Then my mother started doing dishes. My mother always does dishes when she's upset. But after a while she seemed to forget she was upset, and she started singing a Billie Holiday song. My mom loves Billie Holiday, and she can imitate her to a tee.

We don't know what Woolsey's father will do. We know he'll get up, wheel himself into the kitchen, turn on the radio, and fry up some eggs before he goes to wake up Woolsey. After that it's a wild card. We did leave a note on the bed. But we're not sure how Woolsey's dad will react to it, so we need to get out of town soon. Really soon. Right away, in fact.

*Chapter Eleven*

*I* actually start floating off the sidewalk when I see the little red car and Riley in his Bob Dylan sunglasses and that torn tuxedo jacket and his favorite flannel shirt. (I have *all* Riley's shirts memorized — the brown one, the green one, the red checked one.) He's driving along with one hand on the wheel, slouching back in his seat, singing "Girl of the North Country" at the top of his lungs at six in the morning. As I'm standing at the curb, the wind is warm and gentle like a big soft cat rolling against me.

We've been kind of hiding outside of Elsie's Roast Beef, trying to keep out of sight — Elsie's Roast Beef, where you can practically get a whole cow on a sandwich. Woolsey, in fact, has talked the early morning prep cook into selling him one (even though Desmona and I disapprove), and he's looking cheerful about it, in spite of the fact that he's worried about sneaking out of town without telling his dad.

"I have to eat, Rachel," he says, looking at me with those sheepish Woolsey eyes. "I mean, how else am I going to grow? I can't stay short forever. I couldn't live with myself." (Anyway, it's a good thing he's tanking up because when Woolsey is hungry, he drives everybody crazy.)

When I get in the little backseat of the car, I'm smelling lilacs and I'm floating. I have wind in my sleeves and in my skirt. I'm floating above Cambridge. I can see the Charles River winding like a little ribbon draped across a table. Now I'm in the clouds.

Desmona says, "You look really happy, Rachel. Are you missing a test this week at school or something? I shouldn't be doing this at all today. If the big G hadn't locked me in, I would be at the pound walking dogs."

"No one exactly twisted your arm," says Riley. Desmona blows a kiss toward Riley as if she's blowing smoke in his face, and we take off in the car. We drive through a whole swarm of white petals blowing over the road. Petals fly up all around us, some even landing in my lap.

Looking in his rearview mirror, Riley says, "Hey, Rachel, you've got petals in your hair." And I smile. There are delicate purple flowering trees leaning against brownstones on this street. They are shy and flirtatious, bending their arms against the walls.

Des puts her feet up on the dashboard. She's wearing irreverent white ankle socks and gold lamé sandals. Riley has on his suede cowboy boots. They are cracked and worn and have never looked the same since he walked into a swimming pool with them on last fall.

Riley revs the motor, and we fly through more petals. Then we hear a siren. It's coming right up behind us, red and loud. Woolsey rolls his eyes.

Des says, "Do you think Burns will miss me while I'm suspended?" The siren grows louder and louder, and then a big police car rolls past us, chasing something invisible on the horizon.

We zip over the Charles River and sail up into the sky. Riley has our whole trip planned. He's still driving with one hand on the steering wheel, holding a map of Massachusetts with the other, and we're all singing along with Bob Dylan, who Riley is always telling us is really named Bobby Zimmerman.

"How does he get all these facts?" Desmona says, throwing her arms up into the wind.

Riley looks over his shoulder toward the back-seat. He's checking out the Woolsey situation, looking for something to poke him about. Woolsey looks back cheerfully and says, "What?"

And Riley goes, "Oh, nothing, Alfred. I was just wondering how you were taking all this."

"I'm taking it on the chin," says Woolsey, standing up on his seat, arms out like an airplane. "Look! Up in the sky. It's a bird. It's a plane. It's Superman!" shouts Woolsey.

"Come on, Woolsey, grow up," says Des. "And sit down. You're rocking the boat."

Riley swivels his head around again and smiles that smile that rolls through me like the wind. It's a complicated smile, layers I could analyze like my mom does now that she's taken that psychology class. Every dream I tell her, she'll write down. Then she'll ask, "Were there two windows or three windows in the house in your dream? Were the windows open or closed? Was the house big or small?" My mom sees everything as symbolic, but then she'll never tell me what she's figured out or what any of it means.

If I were to analyze Riley's smile, I'd say it's a mixture of warmth with a little touch of doubtfulness, a little twinge of inwardness. He isn't always easy to figure out. There are things he won't talk about at all. For instance, when Desmona brings up their mother, a lot of the time Riley just walks away.

Riley used to play basketball. Two years ago, he was the youngest boy on the varsity team. The night of the important game between Cambridge Latin and Boston Latin, the coach bought a big bouquet of roses. Before the game started, each team player was supposed to take a single rose to his mother in the bleachers. But Riley's mother wasn't there that night.

When Riley got home, there were two policemen in the living room. Desmona pushed by them and ran upstairs and got under her bed and wouldn't come out.

The next day they dredged Walden Pond. They found Desmona and Riley's mother lying on the bottom in a white dress, holding a notebook full of her poems. There were pages and pages from that notebook floating like flowers on the surface of Walden Pond.

If I were to analyze Riley's smile, I would say it's multilayered, cuts through time. It could be Romeo's smile. It could be the elfish smile of Puck from *A Midsummer Night's Dream.* It's one of those smiles you can analyze and analyze and analyze, but you can never quite figure it out.

Woolsey is still standing up on the seat of the car, every inch of him blowing in the wind, all his clothes fluttering, singing—his hair, his mouth, even his eyes, everything swept back by the force of the car riding along.

"You know what you need, Alfred? You need to jump-start your social life," says Riley, smiling that mile-long going-forever smile.

"What?" says Woolsey. "What? Don't you remember I'm the guy who made it into Club 47 the night Bob Dylan was reported to be there? Remember I got in because my cousin works in the kitchen? Remember?"

"Sure, I remember," says Riley, "but you still need to jump-start your social life."

"You've got to be kidding," says Woolsey. "I'm the guy who was in Club 47 when the rest of you were waiting outside, lost in a line in the rain. And then, to top it all off, Dylan takes a picture of me."

"Yeah, but you were carrying out the garbage at the time," says Desmona.

"Yeah, well, next time it will be different," says Woolsey. "Next time I'll be dressed all in black. I'll go up to Bob Dylan, and I'll say, 'Zimmerman, I like your work. You're okay.'"

From where I'm sitting, Woolsey really does look like he's flying, with the clouds coming up and running over the top of the sky, with everything sailing away above him. Desmona's up on her knees in the front seat. She's opening a big newspaper that makes a tremendous clatter in the wind. "Look at this elephant, Woolsey," she shouts. "Sit down and look at this elephant. How can you fly like Superman when there's an elephant suffering like this?"

Woolsey's getting more and more giddy, gulping air and jumping around. He isn't listening at all. "Okay, Riley, tell him what we've got in the trunk," says Desmona.

"What?" says Woolsey. "What trunk?"

"Tell him," says Des. "Tell Rachel. Tell them what we've got in our trunk."

"Well," says Riley. "Okay, are you guys ready for this? We've actually got five bushels of apples and thirty bags of carrots in the trunk right now."

"What?" says Woolsey. "What the heck for?"

Desmona tilts her head, pulls a strand of hair away from her mouth, scrunches up her face, and says, "One great thing. One wonderful great deed. It's really everyone's obligation. After that—fine, anything goes. But all of us in the world should be responsible for one extraordinary contribution, whatever it may be."

"What are you talking about?" says Woolsey. "What's that got to do with thirty bags of carrots?"

"Well, I've been thinking and thinking. I've been especially thinking about my mother, how I should have rescued her, but I was too complacent—I was a happy, spoiled child, a child of money. I will *never* be that child again. I will never be complacent again. That is why, Woolsey, we are going to Lock-well, Mass., to rescue this elephant tonight after it gets dark."

"You're joking," says Woolsey, sliding down flat on the seat. "You're joking, absolutely, completely."

"No," says Riley. "She really isn't. She is *not* joking." Then he leans over, turns the volume way up on his tape machine, and Mr. Bob Dylan sobs and wails with us as we roll along, headed straight toward the sky.

# Chapter Twelve

*L*ockwell is a run-down city where everything seems to be toppling over or rusting, and no one seems to know about the exact location of the zoo. We actually have trouble finding anyone who has even *heard* of the zoo. Finally, Riley pulls up next to a police car and asks directions.

The policeman says, "Not really a zoo. There's Westwood Park, which used to be a zoo. Maybe they do have a few animals."

We finally locate Westwood Park, and now we are walking in on the paved road through the grounds, which are quiet and feel abandoned, with paper and cans strewn around in the ferns and bushes.

As we're walking in, Woolsey looks at me and Desmona and says, "You know that song, *Wild Man, your love is tearing me apart,* by the Candles?"

"Yeah," Des goes.

"Well, from now on I want to be called *Wild Man,*" says Woolsey.

Des and I look at each other. She frowns at me, and I frown back. It's midafternoon, too early to do anything except scope out the situation. I just keep thinking we aren't really going to do anything. Desmona isn't really serious. Maybe she's just putting on another show. Maybe she just wants to visit the elephant, feed it some carrots, and leave.

As we wind along the road, I slip to the back of the group the way I usually do. In all of Desmona's and Riley's escapades, I've always tried to be as invisible as possible. I guess I'm the kind of person who prefers to stand in a corner of a room rather than in the very center, avoiding all sorts of things, like blame.

I am watching the three of them ahead of me — Riley with his hand on Des's shoulder, Woolsey leaping along beside them. I'm remembering the first time I met Desmona and Riley. I was trying to walk up the steps at Cambridge High and Latin, but these kids in black leather jackets were coming toward me, ready to start making fun of me again. That's when Desmona and Riley sort of appeared out of nowhere, drifted in between me and them. Riley started saying what a beautiful day it was, and Des was twirling around and around, looking up at the sky with her head thrown back and her arms out, saying, "Oh, it's so pretty. What a pretty blue sky."

That was all it took—the kids in leather jackets kind of melted away. Afterward, Desmona said to me, "So what's your name?"

And I said, "It's Rachel Townsend."

And she went, "This is my brother, Riley. He's a junior. You may have seen him on the basketball team two years ago. He quit because he thinks it's completely idiotic and I agree, don't you?"

When I went to have lunch that day, I was planning to sit alone, the way I usually do, when this small, frail girl named Darcy came over and held out her ghostly little hand and said, "Won't you have lunch with us?"

They were serving chicken that day, and I had a yellow drumstick rolling around on the plate on the tray in front of me. When I sat down at the table and picked up my drumstick, everyone looked at me with these quiet, staring eyes. And Desmona said, "Did you know a chicken like this has spent its whole life in a tiny, horrible cage with nowhere to stand? Chickens like to put their feet on flat surfaces. They have no flat surface, only bars for a floor. Their feet fall through. They are miserable. How can you eat something like that?"

I put the drumstick down and everyone on the other side of the table started clapping and cheering, and I got the feeling that they were clapping and cheering for all the animals that would not die because one more person in the world had just become a vegetarian.

Woolsey turns around now and goes, "Come on, Rachel, we've got to hurry. Riley wants to get over to Christina's house before dark. We aren't going to be here for long."

I breathe a sigh of relief. It sounds like Desmona's changed her mind. For the last hour, I've been so nervous, I felt like I had a bird trapped in my throat.

We pass a man on the road who looks like a park attendant; he is wearing a blue suit with an emblem on the pocket. Desmona goes right up to him. She says, "Hi, nice day."

And he goes, "You bet."

Then Des says, "When does this park close?"

And the attendant says, "Oh, around eight or so tonight. Sundown, I guess. You kids have got plenty of time. It's only three."

"Do you lock the gates at night?" says Desmona. Woolsey nudges her, and Riley looks up at the sky, twiddling his thumbs.

The attendant looks back with his eyebrows tilted, like two twigs forming a tent. "Why are you asking a question like that?" he says.

"Oh, I'm writing a paper for school," says Desmona.

Woolsey is about to throw his hands over Desmona's mouth to keep her from saying anything else, but she goes on. "Is there an elephant here, and where is it kept at night?" And then she adds, "I don't need to be taking notes for the paper I'm writing, because I have a photographic memory."

"Oh," says the attendant.

"Yeah, if I need to remember something, I just flip through my mind like a photo album till I come to the right page." This cracks Riley up. He loves Desmona's jokes. He turns his head toward the trees and tries to laugh without making any noise. Woolsey is quivering all over. His ears are pink. His cheeks are red.

"Well, good luck with your paper. I'm off duty

now," says the attendant, pushing his bicycle forward.

"Anybody else on duty?" calls Des. "Anybody on duty at night? Tonight?"

The guard looks back, his head tilted, his eyebrows two twigs forming a tent.

## Chapter Thirteen

"Come on," says Desmona. "We needed to know all that, didn't we?"

"Why didn't you just tell him what we're planning to do?" says Woolsey, kicking a stone off into the bushes. "*Are* we planning to do anything? Maybe we're going to call it all off."

"Well, look for yourself," says Desmona. We're sitting on a cement block in front of Mandy the elephant. "How can you live the rest of your life leaving this elephant suffering here?" And then she whispers, "One great thing. One extraordinary contribution."

Desmona is right about the park. It's a wreck. The grass grows high along the old cement sidewalks. There are statues that have fallen off their pedestals and lie among tangled bushes. There are rusty ornate archways leading nowhere and an old tilting merry-go-round that plays an out-of-tune, tinny melody.

Desmona sits in front of Mandy the elephant trying to get her attention. The elephant is tied by a short chain to a stake, and she rocks on that chain, back and forth, back and forth, her eyes crazy with longing. Desmona rocks with her, back and forth, tears like rain rolling down her cheeks. She offers the elephant a carrot, but Mandy turns away, rocking, rocking. Nothing will make her stop. Nothing will make her look at us.

After a while, Riley gets up and runs in the wind toward the sad old merry-go-round. "Come on, Rachel," he calls. "Let's ride this old thing." And he jumps on a white horse, his red hair blowing out behind him like fire.

I get on a black horse just behind him, and we ride around and around, me all the while imagining that my horse might catch up to Riley's horse if I could just ride faster, faster, faster. We can see Woolsey running across the park in the distance with two little kids chasing a big orange ball. We can hear their shouts sailing in the wind.

There's almost no one here, nothing here, just Mandy chained to a stake, the merry-go-round, and a short string of cages full of scruffy, sad small animals — a coyote, some monkeys, and a cage full of rabbits.

Riley slides off his horse and leaps in the wind back toward Desmona, leaving me riding alone, around and around on my black horse. Oh, if I could only write a piece of music about this windy, lonely park full of longing — Mandy's longing, her rocking on her chain, back and forth as if she has somewhere she has to be and can't be, can't be because of that chain. And my longing, too, my longing like the wind, like a black horse racing in the wind.

Later in the day at the other end of the park, we find a man selling popcorn. Riley buys a bag for me and another one for Des. Woolsey comes rushing up, breathless, out of control, bumps right into me, and knocks half the popcorn out of my hand. It falls and scatters on the cement like galaxies, constellations, Mr. Krimms's starry maps. Oh, Mr. Krimms, if I could write a piece of music about this park, this wind.

It's getting dark. We take the popcorn back to Desmona. She will not leave the elephant. All afternoon she has been sitting there, coaxing and talking to Mandy.

"I got her to eat a carrot," Desmona says, looking up at us as we hand her the popcorn. "*And* I made eye contact with her finally. She *looked* at me."

"Desmona," says Riley, "we have to go now. We have to go to Christina's summerhouse. It was part of the deal. It's only ten minutes from here. We can't stay here till closing time. We'll come back at midnight."

"What did you say?" says Woolsey, looking at Riley with that dented-can look he gets.

"Hey, Wild Man, you're not afraid of anything, are you?" says Riley to Woolsey.

And Woolsey goes, "Well, no, not exactly." Dented can. Smushed can, eyes rolling around.

"Did you check the back of the park?" says Desmona. "Do you think we can lead the elephant out that way?"

And Riley says, "Yup. I went all through there. It's full of brambles and thorns, but we can get out that way. There are some old fences, but they're all broken."

"You've got to be kidding," says Woolsey. "That elephant must weigh a ton at least. What are you going to do with it?"

"Come on, Des," says Riley, pulling her up to her feet with both hands, and then, since they are already holding two hands, Desmona and Riley suddenly break into the jitterbug—spinning and dancing and doing fancy turns and kicks. From here they look like something straight off *American Bandstand.*

*Chapter Fourteen*

We left the park at about six o'clock in the evening. Woolsey was starving, so we drove around in the downtown area until we found a diner. Now it's nighttime, and we're finally heading into North Lockwell, Massachusetts, the next town over, where Christina's summerhouse is.

"Look at the difference between these two towns," says Desmona, throwing her head back against the seat. "Talk about complete opposites. Unfair or what?" North Lockwell seems to be a fancy ocean resort town, but it's off-season so the little shops near the water are boarded up. We drive around through tall clipped and shaped hedges that look strange, like dark pointed blocks in the night.

Riley pulls up in front of a huge Victorian house with an elaborate wraparound porch. But it's all dark and vacant-looking. "Here we are," he says. "This is Christina's summer place."

"Well, Riley," says Des, "we can see very clearly she's not here. It's still spring—off-season. No one's here."

"I wouldn't be so sure," says Riley, cranking on the hand brake. He climbs out of the car, tossing his long legs over the door, not bothering to open it.

"Woolsey," says Desmona, "when you fall in love, I hope you never act this stupid."

And Woolsey says, "Not a chance. I'm already in love, and I haven't done anything stupid yet."

Des and I look at each other. Eyes wide, mouths shut.

Riley hunches down and tiptoes up to the gate, clicks it open, and crosses the front lawn like the stealthy Pink Panther. We follow him up onto the large creaking porch. The ocean crashes not far away—just beyond the side steps off the porch. We can't see it—we can just hear it roaring in the darkness with the wind in the trees above us and a lighthouse bell clanging in the distance.

We put our faces to the murky window glass and look into the enormous living room, which is empty except for a few chairs and couches draped in white sheets. There's a great mirror above the fireplace, and we can see ourselves reflected, peering in, in the shadows.

"Riley, give it up," says Desmona. "She's not here. We're way too early. No one's here at all."

The wind rushes in the leaves and the ocean crashes. All around us are these huge closed-up empty houses sitting among clipped hedges. One big house on the prow of the hill is completely black except for a faint yellow light in one little window on the third floor. We sit on the wide, windblown steps overlooking the ocean that we can't see.

"How long do you think we should wait before we go back?" says Desmona.

"I don't think we should go back," says Woolsey. "I can't get into any more trouble. The social worker will take me away from my dad. My dad needs me. He thinks he's still in Normandy. He can't get past the beaches of Normandy, France."

"As soon as the moon rises above the clouds," says Riley. "*That's* when we'll go back."

The four of us sit on Christina's ocean steps, waiting for the moon to sail over the clouds. We sit there listening to the lighthouse bell, warning the boats offshore of land and danger, clanging back and forth, back and forth.

# Chapter Fifteen

Westwood Park seemed crummy and broken-down and small by day. By night it is huge, and the road in seems endless (we parked the car in one of the lots and are on foot now). Riley's in the lead with the flashlight sweeping the pines above. They are dark and seem to hover over us like lonely giants with waving arms.

"This feels dangerous," says Woolsey.

And Des says, "It's exciting. Don't you really feel alive right now? You're not bored. You're not sleepy. You're alive."

"I hope so," says Woolsey. "And I'd like to stay that way. My dad needs me."

"We know that, Woolsey," says Riley.

I put my arm on Woolsey's back and say, "Wool, if we make it out alive on this one, I'll buy you a maple walnut cone at Schrafft's in the Square tomorrow, okay?"

"Deal," says Woolsey, shivering.

"No," says Desmona, "that's not good enough. You're settling for too cheap. Riley, what will we do for Woolsey if he makes it through all this in one piece?"

"Hmmm," says Riley, "how about we take Woolsey and his dad to Fenway Park to a Red Sox game? No, seriously. I mean it."

Soon we see the lopsided merry-go-round ahead, stopped dead on its tilted, faded tracks. The horses are still laughing. Their teeth are terrible and shining white in the run-down Lockwell moonlight. A scrawny cat leaps off the merry-go-round and falls into the long grass and disappears.

Woolsey says, "Spooky."

We pass the mangy coyote in his dirty cage. He's up on his skinny legs, his thin hair standing high on his back. He bares his teeth, mirroring the merry-go-round horses. He growls and picks his way through pieces of food thrown around in his cage.

The monkeys are screaming, hanging from poles in the darkness of their cages.

The elephant is in the next cage over now, rocking in there, back and forth, back and forth. A thin chain with a lock holds her cage shut, and Desmona picks up the chain, rolls it in her hands. "This place is disgusting. All these animals are suffering. Who's in charge here?" She shakes the metal lock. "What are we going to do about this, Riley?" Desmona says.

Riley has his Boy Scout pocketknife with him. He folds out a long pointed delicate hook and sticks it in the big old lock; he turns it quietly back and then forward, all the while looking at me.

"I'm not a criminal, Rachel. I learned how to do this the summer I went to basketball camp. So much for basketball," he says, throwing his head back and popping open the lock.

The moonlight falls on his face, making his cheeks gaunt—his hair curly and dark. He looks like an El Greco painting, all shimmery and blue, and look what he's done. The door of the rusty elephant cage creaks open.

"Oh my God," says Desmona. "Oh my God." She slips through the gate slowly. "There, there, girl. We came to save you." She reaches in her pocket for an apple and hands it to the elephant. This time the elephant takes it with her trunk shyly, trustingly.

And Woolsey starts to whimper. "Oh, boy, Desmona. Oh, man alive."

"Tickets and a limo," Riley whispers, "really and truly. A doubleheader even."

We lead the elephant slowly out of the cage. The monkeys begin screaming louder and louder. Woolsey puts his hands over his ears. Gently, quietly, we creep along with the elephant on a rope. Louder and louder the monkeys shriek and chatter. What are they saying?

My ankle gives out from under me, and I fall in the wet grass, down, down into the slippery blackness, suddenly remembering how it was when I was eleven and twelve. I was pretty skinny, pretty shy, never said *boo*, going to school. Kids could sense something. They knew something was wrong. It showed like a broken leg or a broken arm. They started calling me names. All alone. Very, very quiet. Red sneakers. No psychic spot.

Riley pulls me up out of the grass, startles me out of my memory. His hands are warm around my wrists. His breath rolls over my face, his hair a lion's mane in the darkness.

We follow Desmona in the moonlight, making our way out of the woods, the elephant swaying on a long sturdy rope, crunching her way through the underbrush. In the distance, through the dark woods, we can still hear the monkeys screaming, "Thieves! Thieves! Liars!"

# Chapter Sixteen

We've crossed yards. We've taken alleys and backstreets, and we've gone several miles, not far from the open highway. The wind is blowing the tall grass out here near the road, making a sighing, breathing sound. We haven't been talking much. We've just been walking and walking, trying to get as far away from Lockwell as we can before dawn.

Now Desmona is singing to the elephant, leading her along through the tall grass.

*Low, low, breathe and blow,*
*Wind of the western sea!*

Riley picks up the tune with his harmonica, filling the air around us with a sad, lonely lullaby.

We cross a wide field of bleached grass in front of Big Bill's Furniture Warehouse, an abandoned tin building with a partially crumpled roof. There is broken glass everywhere and a big cavernous hole in front for a door. We stop for a minute on the broken cement parking lot. We turn back and look at the highway, full of streams of car lights, and at the stars glittering above like rhinestones in the darkness.

"Come on," says Desmona, "let's go in here." Of all of us, Desmona is the least afraid of the size of the elephant. She gives her a carrot, and the elephant nods her head up and down, her big wide ears shivering and rippling. Mandy was scared at first and pulled back a little on her rope, but now she follows and obeys us, gently doing what she has been trained to do since she was a baby.

We walk through the huge dented doorway of Big Bill's Furniture Warehouse. Inside there is more broken glass and lines of partially burned brocade gold couches that are singed black and bulging open with stuffing and springs. There are rows and rows of them in the huge expanse inside the warehouse.

"Look at this one," says Woolsey, sitting in a gold brocade chair. "It's not too burned. It still looks usable, comfortable, too."

"Come on, Woolsey," says Riley. "We have to find a safe place for this elephant."

"Rachel," says Desmona, "if we save this elephant from suffering, for the rest of my life I can say to myself, I've *done* something. It won't even matter what the rest of my life is like. And this elephant happens to be a beautiful, well-behaved circus animal. She's just like my horse, and it was wrong for her to suffer at all." Then Desmona throws her arms against the elephant's huge gray body as if trying somehow to hold her. Mandy looks at us with timidity and trust and sadness, bobbing her head up and down.

"There are twenty-five couches here," says Woolsey, "and some of them aren't too bad. You could re-cover them."

The hot night air sweeps across Big Bill's Furniture Warehouse and the tin roof rattles and the smell of old smoke and charred furniture fills the air. There are so many lined-up couches and chairs that when I turn around, the room almost looks like an enormous empty movie theater draped in darkness. We lead the docile elephant across the floor, broken glass crunching under our feet. At the back, we step through a hole in the wall, and we walk behind Big Bill's Furniture Warehouse into the fields on the other side.

"Look," says Riley, "there's a pond down there."

We work our way across the field toward the little pond that floats in the middle of this expanse of long grass, and as we get closer, the moon is floating there on its black soupy surface. Desmona walks along next to the elephant, saying, "Yes, this is the gentlest creature. She has been suffering in that place, locked up tight for too long."

Woolsey says, "Oh, man alive, Desmona."

Riley hands me the long rope, and he sits down at the edge of the pond. Then I feel the elephant moving, and I let the rope go slack and slip through my hands, letting her pull forward toward the pond. Then she plunges into the water, swimming out deeper and deeper, out where the moon lies like a rippling yellow cookie.

In the middle of the shadowy pond, the elephant dips her trunk into the water and lifts it up and then sprays her back. She does it again and again and again. And then, in the dappling interstate moonlight, the stars twinkling like tiny pieces of broken glass strewn across the sky, the elephant heaves herself up out of the water and trumpets and trumpets and trumpets.

# Chapter Seventeen

On the other side of the field, we have found a small wood with paths running through it, cigarette butts strewn along among the trails. Old trees carved with graffiti line the paths. Hearts. Daggers. Dates. Initials. We have found an area where the ground sinks into a kind of hollow, a protected area where I'm guessing motorcycle gangs sometimes meet, since we see motorcycle tracks everywhere. There are remnants of a campfire down in the center of this depression, and we have brought Mandy here and continue to feed her apples and carrots. She grazed all night in the darkness on the straw grass at the edge of the woods and drank pond water that we carried up for her in an old bucket we found in the bushes.

Riley has gone out for supplies. He has parked his car in a factory parking lot not too far away, and he has gone back for it now with his hair under a baseball cap, wearing sunglasses.

We're waiting for him in the heat of the woods with the elephant. Sometimes we hear a stray siren from the highway below coming in on the wind. But otherwise, we could be anywhere, in any woods. We could be in the outback in Australia. We could be lost in Vermont. We could be on the moon.

Last night, Riley and Woolsey went back to Big Bill's Furniture Warehouse and carried out a couple of the less-burned brocade couches. Woolsey is sleeping on one of them, curled up like a little boy with his dusty bare feet lying against each other like two small rabbits.

Desmona is awake talking to Mandy, watching her delicately pick up the tiniest little pieces of apple with her trunk. I've been asleep on the ground with my head on Riley's jacket. When I wake up, Desmona tells me I have a crease on my cheek in the shape of a button. "You've got a print of Riley's jacket and button on your cheek," she says.

And I think to myself, *That figures.*

As I lie here, I wonder about my parents at home. They must know by now that I'm gone. What will they do? Will they go to the police? Will they cry? What will they say about me? Will my father stand by the window looking down at the cars on the street below the way he usually does when he's upset? Will my mother wash the dishes, repeating over and over again to my father, "I was out. You were watching her. What time did she leave?" My father will surely see the note we left at Woolsey's. Doesn't he visit Sergeant Pontiac every day to make sure he has everything he needs? What will my parents do when they read the note? How will they go about finding us since they have no idea which way we went?

The hot quiet air makes me think about my dad playing his saxophone on weekends, how he used to get crummy jobs on a Saturday night at, say, the Park Lounge playing with a background band. Sometimes he was part of a trio that played for wedding parties out in Needham and Natick. The problem was he wasn't able to make any money at it. Originally he thought he would move to Boston to play music, so he took on the superintendent job at 87 Brattle temporarily. He tried to practice on

Saturday afternoons down in our apartment, but someone invariably telephoned and complained. He had to go downtown to the Boston Common to practice his saxophone somewhere out under a tree in the park. Sometimes he took me. I made paper boats to sail on the little pond there. Paper boats. Some of them were quite elaborate, but all of them sank. Every one.

Sometimes, in the Public Garden, my father paid for me to ride with all the tourist children on the swan boats. They were so excited to be with their parents and grandparents, while I was alone, waving good-bye to my father, who stood under a tree practicing his saxophone, trying to find a moment of time to work on what it was he loved to do.

Slowly my dad quit trying to play saxophone, and I guess that must have disappointed my mother. But it was hard enough for him to deal with all that goes wrong on a good day in a big tall apartment building. Something always goes awry—a key won't work, a window gets stuck—it's always something.

Through most of the years I lived in that apartment building, I was the only kid there, except for the ninety-two-year-old Butterfield sisters' great-grandnieces who came at Christmastime in red-

and-green outfits. They monopolized the birdcage elevator, screaming and squealing down the elevator shaft and bouncing a great white ball in the polished tile foyer so that it ripped to the ceiling and ricocheted off the walls. My father chuckled about them, was lenient and easy and let them do as they wished. Everything was for the tenants—his time and his attention and maybe even a little of his love. I suppose that disappointed my mother too. She had wanted him to be a jazzman, and slowly he became father to a whole building of people—lost in all their needs.

Yes, I was the only kid who lived in the building until Woolsey moved in, yet I never noticed him. I thought he might be younger than me, and he never quite came into focus. Although he and Sergeant Pontiac came to our Thanksgiving dinner every year. We always invited all the shut-ins and all the lonely tenants to our Thanksgiving. Sergeant Pontiac was very quiet in those days. He never said much of anything at all.

Because she didn't have any relatives, Mrs. Ethel Elgar, who taught a class at Radcliffe called The Life of the Fruit Fly, was also invited. She brought me a book one time that told the story of silkworms and how silk is made. The book was full of pictures of all these delicate cocoons like little lanterns hanging from branches.

At those Thanksgivings, Woolsey would be there with his father, his head just barely peeking over the tabletop. I remember only his glasses reflecting the candlelight and the way he loved walnuts and was cracking them like crazy on the table after dinner. We always had Thanksgiving dinner, Christmas dinner, Easter dinner, for anyone in the building who had nowhere to go.

It kind of seems to me that my parents and I were never alone together after a while as a family, all three of us—never on holidays anyway. Other times it would be me and my dad while my mom worked, or me and my mom while my dad was out in the hallways and kitchens and crawl spaces of the building, somewhere at all hours, even in the middle of the night sometimes. Maybe that also disappointed my mother—the way he was always immersed, involved in fixing broken things that were anywhere but in our apartment.

In my room at night there has always been a shadow on the wall. In summer, fall, winter, and spring the shadow flickers. I can never figure out which tree or roof next-door is causing it—where the shadow comes from. I try moving my bed, but it is always there anyway, like a dark gnarled hand waving at me.

Riley's been gone longer than we expected. I've been asleep, and when I sit up my head starts to spin and I see the scraggly woods above us flickering and dancing in the heat. I'm thirsty, and I can tell when I look at Desmona, sitting there next to Woolsey and the elephant, that things are getting uneasy. I can tell when I look at Desmona's face that she feels scared. She looks like she's about to say, "I don't know how we're going to get out of this one alive." Her feet are bare and covered in soft dry dust.

Woolsey is covered with dust, too. There are patches of it on his cheek, and it's on his legs up to his knees, like a long pair of socks. I can tell by looking at both of them that they are worried. Riley hasn't gotten back yet. He may have been caught. We're thirsty and tired of eating carrots and apples.

"I know a man who turned orange and croaked from drinking carrot juice every day," says Woolsey. "I think we shouldn't eat any more carrots."

"Oh, Woolsey," says Desmona. "Don't worry so much. It could be stunting your growth."

"Well, it's true," says Woolsey.

We should have thought of bringing water. I eyed the pond earlier, but when I looked at the reeds and moss rippling with industrial clouds above, I decided against it. We sit there, the three of us knowing we can't get out of this easily, knowing if Riley doesn't come back, we're sunk. We can hear the cars on the highway rushing and swooshing and honking in the distance.

Mandy stirs. She gets to her feet and curls her long trunk toward the bag of apples. I step back a little as she moves forward because she's so huge and I haven't really gotten used to standing that close to her yet. Woolsey straightens the chain around the tree. The links are loose. The rope is frayed.

Mandy picks up dirt and dust with her trunk and throws it on her back.

"Don't do that, Mandy," says Woolsey. "I just took you down to the pond for a bath. We have to wait till night to go again, so stop throwing dirt on your back."

"They're supposed to do that. Haven't you ever heard of a dust bath? Oh, where is he?" says Desmona. "He's got to come through. He's got to come back."

It's getting toward noon. The air is still and hot. No sign of Riley.

Desmona is sitting there braiding a wreath of lilacs for Mandy's neck. She doesn't look up but braids the stems in and out. "My mother's favorite flowers were lilacs," she says. "I would have done something for her. I would have rescued her, but I was too little. I didn't know how." Desmona sounds weak, as if the heat and fatigue are beginning to get to her.

At a quarter to two I'm falling into a hazy drifting sleep again. Suddenly, Woolsey says, "There he is. Whoopee! I see him! We're saved!" Woolsey leaps up off the couch, stuffing and dust flying all around him.

And, yes, it's true, I can see, way in the distance, Riley's red baseball cap coming through the long, brittle grass. He stirs his arm around in the air, waving. He's got a big bag of something and what looks like a shiny blue bullhorn in his hands.

"Just in time, Mr. Red," says Desmona to herself.

"I didn't see any police cars out by the warehouse parking lot, but there were a couple of them a few blocks down on the side of the road. They didn't notice me. I went right into the grocery store and got a bunch of cookies and candy. Hope you guys like M&M's," says Riley, tossing a bag at me.

I'm so tired that everything is looking a little strange just now. There are flies or bees buzzing in the air, and there is the sweet smell of lilacs. The afternoon heat is making everything seem to shimmer, even Riley. He shimmers and wavers as he talks.

"Riley, where's the water?" says Woolsey.

"Oh, that?" says Riley. "Well, I got two six-packs of soda." He sets the cartons on the soft fluffy dust. "And a carton of lemonade for Des."

Then he reaches into the bag with his long red-freckled arm, and he leaves it there, saying, "Woolsey, this is going to rattle your brains a little, but I think ultimately you will be pleased as I know my sister will be." He looks over at me, and my eyes fall into the green ponds of light that are Riley's eyes. "I think Rachel will be . . . a little disconcerted however . . ."

He then draws two newspapers from the bag — the *Lockwell Times* and the *North Lockwell Journal.* The *Lockwell Times* says in huge black letters, ELEPHANT

ESCAPES FROM WESTWOOD PARK PETTING ZOO. DANGEROUS AND UNPREDICTABLE. Riley reads the article aloud, which states that the elephant disappeared at around ten or eleven at night. No guard was on duty. Some people had seen "an unsavory group of teenagers near the site at closing time. Law enforcement officers are combing the area. People in the surrounding vicinity are to keep children in. If the elephant is sighted anywhere, contact police or National Guard."

"Unsavory teenagers?" says Woolsey, looking down at his dust-covered feet.

"What about the 'dangerous elephant' part?" says Desmona, sitting up and patting Mandy's trunk. "This is an old trained circus elephant. A small female. There's *nothing* dangerous about her. Nothing."

"Yeah, but what will my social worker say when she gets wind of this?" says Woolsey. "I mean, Desmona, you've really done it now. We'll probably get shot. The police will shoot us."

"Nah, nah," says Riley. "That's why we're putting up this metal barricade. We're going to have protection. They can't shoot through corrugated metal—relax, Woolsey."

"And we've got this bullhorn, Pontiac. We're going to make our demands with this bullhorn," says Desmona.

And Woolsey says, "Desmona, don't call me Pontiac."

# Chapter Eighteen

Amazingly, it's night again and the police haven't found us. Late in the afternoon, a small boy about six years old appeared on the grassy hill just above us. Riley put his first two fingers to his mouth and gestured "shush" to the boy and waved to him. We could hear his mother shouting in the background. "Sebastian. Sebastian. Come here right now." Sebastian stood there a long time, the wind blowing through his shirt like a sail, and then suddenly he just took off.

Now we are completely alone with the darkness and the fear. Soon enough they will find us. But we have built a flimsy tin wall around us. Woolsey has found some big pieces of plastic here and there, and he has been working on making a little tent for himself. We also have plenty of soda and cookies and apples.

Desmona is lying on a couch looking up at the darkness. She's humming and whistling in a sing-song kind of way, and then suddenly she says, "What happened that day? Why? If I close my eyes, I can remember every minute of the day my mother died. That morning she said she couldn't come to my school because she was going on a picnic. Why would anyone go on a picnic by themselves? Why would she be in a boat all alone?"

"Desmona, could we change the subject?" says Riley. "Do you have to remember so much?"

"I can't help it. I can remember everything. But you can't remember anything about our mother," says Desmona.

"Oh, sure I can remember," says Riley. "I have this memory of ice-skating inside the conservatory in the winter. It was kind of crazy. I think she flooded the whole place with a hose so we could skate in there. We had this weird indoor ice-skating rink. She did it because the public rink was closed and *you* wanted to ice-skate."

"I can't believe you said that, Riley. That's the

first memory of our mother you have admitted to," says Desmona.

"Can we change the subject now? I mean, what's the point?" says Riley.

Desmona told me once that Riley never cried about his mother—not that night after the basketball game, not the next day, not at the funeral when everyone was rushing around him with food and wine, knocking into him but never knocking him over. He was so staunch, he was like a pillar, so stoic, it was like it had been someone else's mother—a neighbor's brother-in-law's mother or somebody's mother on TV.

"Yes, I remember the day she died," says Desmona. "She packed a picnic. I saw her put in a little sandwich and a piece of fruit and a small thermos of lemonade. My mother never drank lemonade. I should have known something was wrong right then."

Riley rolls on his back and looks up at the sky, the Madman's Hair, the constellation of the Mending Heart. "Desmona, can we change the subject, please? No use trying to answer questions that have no answers," he says.

"Yeah," says Woolsey. "Let's focus on the problem

at hand for a change. What are we going to do with this elephant? Aren't you scared about all this elephant stealing?"

"Nah," says Riley. "I'm not scared to rescue a pitiful elephant. But you know what I'm scared of? I'm scared to ask Christina on a date. I'm scared she'll say no."

"There's a fifty percent chance Christina could say yes," says Woolsey. "You gotta look at the odds."

"I *am* looking at the odds, and there's a fifty percent chance she could say no," says Riley. "That's what I'm talking about."

"I'm looking at the odds that I'm gonna be moving someday because my dad needs to be on the ground floor so he can get out in his wheelchair, but I'd miss you guys," says Woolsey. "My dad wants to move back to Gary, Indiana, where he's from. He says they call Gary the 'Mistake on the Lake.'"

Riley picks up his harmonica and then looks over at me and tugs on my braid. "Rachel, everyone else has talked," he says. "What's *your* secret?"

"Oh, um, well, I used to write piano music and I can't anymore. It's gone," I say.

"She wants to be a composer like Fanny Mendelssohn," says Woolsey.

"Who's that?" says Desmona.

"She was the sister of Felix Mendelssohn. She wrote music, too," says Woolsey. "Rachel wants to be like that—a woman composer someday."

"Yeah, except there's only one little hitch—I can't think of any music anymore, so it will never happen," I say.

"Really? You already play Chopin," says Riley. "That's pretty good for a little kid."

"She's not a little kid, Riley, and neither am I. You don't have to baby-sit for me and my friends. You can leave anytime you want. We're fine, aren't we, Rachel?"

"Okay," says Riley, "I may take you up on that." He starts in playing his harmonica again, and I don't say anything more. *Rilly, rally, ree, I see something you don't see, and the color is red.* My mom's red purse. She's walking away. She's moving through the crowd. She's going in the subway. I'm sitting at the window all alone, looking out at the rain. It pours and pours. No psychic spot. *Rilly, rally, ree, I see something you don't see, and the color is lonely.* Always alone. I try to get my parents together. They aren't talking. I'm doing a survey for school. A questionnaire for homework. You both have to sit down together and answer questions. My first question—why are you two never in the same room at the same time?

Woolsey turns to me and says, "Rachel, you seem sad. Are you okay?"

I look up at the sky and say, "There's Mr. Krimms's constellation, the one he calls the Mending Heart."

"Looks like a broken heart to me," says Desmona.

"No," I say, "see the little line up the middle that looks like stitches? Mr. Krimms says that's the repair."

And Woolsey goes, "She's right. You see that, Des?"

Suddenly, Desmona sits up very quickly and reaches in her jacket pocket. She brings out a tiny stump of a candle and from her other pocket a Japanese lantern that collapses flat when it's not being used. She opens the Japanese lantern like an accordion. Desmona has a whole drawer full of these paper lanterns at home in her room. She buys them in Boston when her father takes her to Chinatown for lunch when he comes home from his business trips. Desmona tells me she always eats Seven Stars and a Moon there because of the "completely poetic name."

Now she hangs the lantern on a bush and sets the candle on a rock just underneath it. "There," she says, "that feels better, doesn't it? Isn't it beautiful?" The lantern glows orange in the darkness. A dreamy, warm wind comes up around us. "You see," says Desmona, "this is what life is for. This is how you keep the sadness away."

And I lie there in the dim light listening to Riley rustling nearby. He's playing his favorite Bob Dylan song again. The tune ripples through me and makes me feel like I'm floating through stars and clouds and moons.

> *Remember me to one who lives there.*
> *She once was a true love of mine.*

He muffles the harmonica in his red Riley knuckles. I know he's thinking about Christina, and I look over at him thinking how incredibly lucky Christina is. She doesn't even know how lucky she is—to be the sweet recipient of this mournful, muffled song. From where I'm resting on the ground, I could reach out and touch Riley's head, his hair, the curve of his nose, his eyebrows. That's how close I am to him. That close.

As I lie here, I remember all those times I went over to the practice rooms at Radcliffe, hoping to write a piece of music. In the music building they have all these pianos in little soundproof rooms. When I found a vacant one, I'd go in there and sit before this big monster of a piano, and in the emptiness of the room, I'd try to make up a melody. But I was like a bird with no voice, a bird that opens its beak and tries to sing but can't. Then I'd look at my hands lying on the keys. They'd look like broken bird wings to me. I'd be thinking all the while, *Where did the music go?*

Then I'd get my books out of my book bag and start practicing Chopin. And as I played a piece, my mind would drift. I'd remember that day one of my father's old friends came to visit. Jim. He used to be one of the Hot Weather Horns from Pittsburgh, Pennsylvania. He brought his old clarinet along, and my dad got out his saxophone and we rode off in Jim's car. My mother came along. She was smiling. Her hair was blowing around, and we drove way out into the country.

I was little, maybe seven years old. We sat in a

pretty field of orange flowers. My mother called them Indian paintbrushes. And my dad and Jim played their horns, and my mom sang. She used to be a jazz singer. While they played and sang, I roamed around in the Indian paintbrushes and cornflowers.

On the way home in the car, my mother said, "Jim, I almost wish you hadn't visited. It kind of makes me feel bad, thinking what we could have done."

"Doesn't pay the rent," my dad said, looking out the window.

# Chapter Nineteen

We've been in the woods for at least a week. I can't believe that we are still here, that we haven't died or starved or been arrested. Some of us are holding up better than others. Mandy, of course, is thriving, but we are worried she isn't getting enough to eat. Riley and Woolsey seem to be okay, too. But Desmona is a wreck. She looks awful. Her clothes are dirty. Her hair is full of leaves, and she's on the edge of falling apart, I think. She's so tired, sometimes she doesn't make sense.

She was walking in the woods earlier reciting Shakespeare's *Othello,* including Burns's comments. "My mother named me after Desdemona in *Othello.*

It was Riley who started dropping the *de* when we were little. My real name is Desdemona," said Desmona. "Can you imagine naming a child after a tragic figure like that?" She was resting her head on Mandy's trunk as she talked. "Why would she give me a name like that? You know, a name really affects you. You know, it shapes your whole being. I mean, if my mother had named me Janet, we probably wouldn't be in this mess. Is it a mess? Are we in a mess?" Then she went on leading Mandy through the woods, reciting more *Othello.*

"With Des I'm not sure what's an act and what's real sometimes. Do you know what I mean?" said Riley, looking at me for reassurance. Riley seems to turn to me for reassurance a lot. Do I think Christina would want to go to a play or a movie? *If she agreed, what kind of movie do I think she would like?*

"Oh, Riley," I ended up saying once, "it hardly matters—she would be with *you*. That's all that's important."

Riley looked at me that time startled, like the way Walden Pond looks when you throw a pebble in it.

∽

The darkness around us is like a velvet glove, warm and full of sweetness. Are there honeysuckles or apple trees blooming nearby? It's gentle like spring, but it's hot and dry like summer. The Japanese lantern glows above the black-and-gold couches. Desmona and Riley are both asleep. Desmona amazes me. I could never save an elephant. I couldn't be doing any of this if it wasn't for Desmona. My mother says I have no mind of my own. "You're just letting these kids sway you like a willow branch caught in a flood. You're more than a willow branch," my mother said. "I'm looking forward to the day you discover that, to the day you walk away your own person." But what does she know?

Nothing. Nothing. Nothing. If I were at home now, I'd go and visit Mr. Krimms. I don't have to tell him things. He knows. He seems to know *everything*, with that large globe sitting there casting a faint blue light. I like the smell of curry and cloves at Mr. Krimms's, and from his little window in the kitchen I can usually see a starling's nest in the tree outside. He calls it *the apartment*. "Looks like the apartment is rented again this year," he'll say, coming out of his bedroom in his soft felt slippers. Last spring, from that window, I could see the mother and father starling taking turns stuffing big tufts of string and hay into the hole. I could see right then that my parents never worked together like that.

"Put it in your music," said Mr. Krimms, looking at me. "Make your hands and heart say it with piano notes."

That's the kind of nice thing about the apartment building. I know all the people living there, and they are more like my family than my family. Mr. Krimms is like a grandfather or a great-uncle or something. He plays beautiful classical concertos on the piano. "Rachel," he'll say to me, "lift with the lilt. Isn't this a pretty piece?" And he'll roll back and forth with the music. The first time Mr. Krimms played for me, I saw the little blue numbers tattooed on his forearm. "It was the music that saved me, Rachel," he said, looking up at me as he played.

It is because of Mr. Krimms that I long to write a nocturne or a sonata. "Nothing ever comes to me," I told him once. "I don't hear melodies anymore."

"You'll hear them in your head again one day," he said to me. "You'll hear the music clear as a bell. And when you do, Rachel, you write it down as fast as you can. Don't put it off. Don't let it get away."

✣ ✣ ✣

Yes, I usually spend more time with Mr. Krimms or Mrs. Ethel Elgar than I do in my own apartment. In fact, if anyone should ever ask me where I live, I could point to the tall brick building shaped like a crescent moon and say, "I live there, in all twelve apartments, sort of." Once, when it was bedtime, my parents couldn't find me. They had to call every apartment in the building. They discovered I was visiting the ninety-two-year-old Butterfield sisters, eating ice cream with them. They were prone to inviting me down to visit, and then one of the sisters would say, "Could you make a trip down to Sage's and get some chocolate ice cream for me, dear?"

And the other sister, who looks just like her, would say, "No, dear, get vanilla, okeydokey?"

And I'd say, "Okeydokey." Then, when I got to Sage's, I never knew which flavor to buy, so I'd get chocolate-and-vanilla swirl and that seemed to please them.

I often run errands for Sergeant Pontiac, too, especially when Woolsey takes swimming lessons at the high school on Saturdays. (He hasn't learned to swim yet, but like he says, at least he's getting comfortable in the water.)

I do all sorts of things for most of the tenants in the building, like changing lightbulbs and rescuing spiders from bathtubs. And one time Mrs. Ethel Elgar dropped a brand-new loaf of bread out of her sixth-floor kitchen window by mistake. I saw it sail by my window on its way down, and then guess who got a phone call and had to go fetch it?

I kind of see all these little worlds behind the apartment door numbers as sort of a three-dimensional Advent calendar. Especially at Christmastime — I get to see all the Christmas trees in all the different apartments and taste all the varieties of cookies and candies.

Woolsey and I went to Inman Square to buy a Christmas tree last year. We dragged it back through Harvard Yard, sweeping the sidewalks and the streets as we pulled it along. It was late in the season, and the man had given us the tree for two dollars, which was great because Woolsey and his dad have to live on small disability checks.

One day Mr. Krimms found out Sergeant Pontiac lived in our building. Mr. Krimms was in a concentration camp somewhere in Europe when Sergeant Pontiac landed with his men in Normandy on D-day. I don't know if Mr. Krimms lost some of his family during the war. There is a framed photograph near his bed of his dark-eyed wife holding a violin as if it were a child. I have never asked him much about her. Mr. Krimms is pretty old—too old to be asked those sorts of questions.

When he found out Sergeant Pontiac lived in our building, Mr. Krimms insisted on visiting him. Woolsey and I weren't sure at all how any of this was going to work out. Mr. Krimms has a Polish accent and tends to get carried away talking about astronomy and music. And Sergeant Pontiac seems to shout a lot and wants to talk about Normandy and the terrible day on the beaches there.

"I must meet him, Rachel," Mr. Krimms said to me that day. "Men like that saved men like me. If not for the Sergeant Pontiacs, it could have gone on forever, the war."

The next day, Mr. Krimms hurried out to Sage's to buy muffins, and he bought one of those big bunches of gladiolas that they sell in buckets around the newspaper stand in Harvard Square. I set the table in Woolsey's apartment with a white tablecloth while Woolsey went down in the birdcage elevator to get Mr. Krimms. When they came to the door, Mr. Krimms's face was lost behind the huge bouquet of gladiolas. They towered above him in oranges and purples.

Woolsey was all excited because he'd never had a party in his apartment before. He was leaping around, eyeing the box of muffins and whistling. Mr. Krimms was wearing a bow tie, and he had a scarf over his shoulders when I opened the door and invited him in.

Sergeant Pontiac wheeled out into the room with great speed and made a cute complete circle in his wheelchair, and then waved and said, "Welcome." He even seemed more dressed up, wearing a clean plaid shirt buttoned all the way up to the neck. "Welcome," he said again, and then he wheeled away with his back to us and looked out toward the curtained window, not saying anything.

Mr. Krimms put the flowers in a jar of water and set them on the table. They fell over on their long stems, like wooden soldiers splayed out across the white tablecloth in pools of water. Mr. Krimms rushed over and picked them up, their stems dripping water all over the rug. I found a bigger vase, and we put them back on the table.

Mr. Krimms said, "Sergeant Pontiac, it's a great honor to meet you. I was one of the broken people dying in a concentration camp when you and your men came to Normandy to save us." Sergeant Pontiac just kept looking out toward the window, his back stiff and silent. "I brought you some muffins, Sergeant Pontiac, and some flowers," said Mr. Krimms.

Chapter Twenty

Desmona looks over at Woolsey and he looks back. "What is that noise?" she says. Then she gets up slowly, looking toward the woods, listening. We hear voices, more than one. They vibrate in and out of range. We hear sticks cracking, leaves swishing. Desmona grabs my arm. We stand there frozen in the woods—dead-still, trembling.

Then we begin to recognize Riley's rolling laugh—he's with someone. Des breathes in and frowns, looking at me and Woolsey. The voices get closer, and then Riley comes bounding into the campsite with Mickey O'Dell. They are babbling on about some guy at some party.

"I kid you not, garçon," Riley is saying. "No,

seriously. I kid you not." Mickey always dresses in black pants and a white shirt, so Riley calls him *garçon* (*waiter* in French).

When he first gets to the campsite, Mickey takes a few steps backward, puts his hands up in the air in front of him as if he's stopping traffic, and says, "Hold everything."

Mickey wants to look cool, but I can tell he can't believe his eyes. He can't believe the charred French parlor room couches. He can't believe the campfire. He can't believe the plastic tent Woolsey has made. Mickey can't believe how messy we look. He can't believe our dirty hands, our fingernails. He can't believe the leaves in Desmona's hair. But most of all he can't believe the elephant.

Mandy goes on eating, swinging her trunk along the ground looking for a stray apple. Then her trunk goes up into the tree above and pulls down a branch. She drops it by her foot, steps on it to hold it in place, and then pulls off pieces and lifts them to her mouth.

Mickey steps back. One step. Two steps. He backs away from the campfire, away from the couches, away from the metal wall we've positioned around us. "Wait a minute," he says. "What's going on here?"

"Hey, garçon," says Riley, "I told you about all this—you weren't listening, man."

"Where in the world did you get that huge elephant? What the hell have you guys been doing?" says Mickey.

We all fall silent for a minute. It's so quiet, all we can hear is Mandy crunching a branch. It's so quiet, all we can hear is the leaves clicking and rattling in the trees above.

"My sister wanted to rescue it," says Riley. "It was really awful—you can't even imagine. Those people were real idiots."

"It was a monstrosity," says Desmona, going over to Mickey and hugging him. "Oh, Mickey, thank you for coming to visit us. We were lonely, weren't we, Riley? These woods are lonely, aren't they, Rachel?"

"I can't stay long," says Mickey, backing up. "Does anybody know about all this?"

Woolsey sticks his head out of the plastic tent and holds out a newspaper. *The* newspaper.

"Whoa," says Mickey. "You guys are making the local front page."

"No kidding," says Woolsey. "We're ruined. Finished. Dead in the water." And then he draws his head back into the tent like a turtle and disappears.

I get pretty shy in these situations. When Riley is with his real friends he seems taller, older, far away. I go over and sit down and lean against Desmona, and she puts her arm over my shoulder and we sit there looking up at Riley and Mickey, me hoping Mickey will think of something to do. Maybe he will make Desmona realize what has happened. Maybe Mickey will help us.

But then Riley goes, "Hey, Mickey, did you listen to that record I left at your place?"

And Mickey goes, "Yeah, I did." And then they start talking about music, calling each song a *cut*. "Did you hear that cut on the record?"

That's when my heart sinks because *nobody* seems to be thinking about what we ought to do with Mandy. My heart sinks because Desmona is smiling, looking up at the sky as if we were sitting on somebody's patio and it was her birthday. She has an it's-my-birthday look about her.

Then I start thinking, *Who can help us? Who?* If Mickey can't help us, maybe somebody else back at home could. What about Darcy? Maybe we could go call her and tell her what has happened. She probably couldn't get away though. She has five younger brothers and sisters, and she has to take care of them a lot.

146

No, I'm sure she can't help. I know because once Desmona took me to Darcy's house in East Cambridge. It was one of those three-decker wooden places, those gray asbestos-shingled tenement buildings with three sloping porches tacked on the front.

We rang Darcy's bell. Des was wearing her Mexican blue-and-pink serape and her red shoes that she had glued glitter all over. We were standing there, me and Des, looking up at the third-floor porch, ringing the bell. Darcy came out on the little porch and looked down.

"Oh, hi, Des," she said.

Des said, "Look at my shoes, Darcy . . . glitter! I glued glitter on them!"

Darcy peered over the edge of the porch. "Oh, Des, just look at you!" she said.

"Come on with us to Walden Pond," said Des. "Riley's driving."

"Oh, I can't," said Darcy. She put her hands together. They looked like little angel wings. (Even so, Darcy can type seventy-five words a minute with those little hands — the best in Desmona's typing class.) "I can't, Des. You know." And then she picked a bunch of dogwood flowers that were blooming in a tree next to her porch, and she tossed them down at our heads — petals, leaves, flowers. "See you at lunch on Monday," said Darcy, disappearing into the third-floor apartment. As we walked away, we turned back and saw her in the window, standing there like a little ghost with two of her small sisters.

No, Darcy can't help us, and it looks like Mickey is leaving now anyway. *Wait, don't go. Come back. Don't leave us. We don't know what to do next. Where should we take the elephant?*

Riley is leading Mickey down the path. "Let's go shoot a little pool. I'll drive you back. Mickey's school is like ten minutes from here, Des. See you guys in a little while," says Riley.

And they go off through the woods, Mickey turning around now and then to look back at Mandy. We watch Riley and Mickey as they dart along the field keeping low and quiet, weaving toward Big Bill's Furniture Warehouse.

When they are gone, a silence settles in. The wind from the highway below, the roar of leaves, the campfire dancing in front of us. Des is whistling and stirring the coals with a stick. "I hope Riley brings back some potatoes. Wouldn't they taste good?" says Des. She has a big smudge of charcoal on her cheek. "Wouldn't it be yummy? Oh, don't you wish you could take a bath? I'm so tired, I wanna go home. I want to go home and find my mother in the kitchen. I want her to be making spaghetti."

"Des, Mickey's right," I say. "What are we going to do next? We have to do *something*."

"Don't ask me any more questions, Rachel. I'm too tired. No, I want my mother to be making lasagna. I can see her layering the noodles in the pan. You have to layer them with cheese."

Just beyond Des, Mandy stands looping her trunk up into the branches and pulling leaves down. She has stripped several trees of their leaves and branches and has eaten all the long grass around the edge of the woods. She is earth-shatteringly enormous, dazzling like a great ocean liner, luminous in her grayness. She is huge and gentle and capable of pulling whole trees up by their roots. But she doesn't. She holds back. She sways her trunk like the arm of an Indian dancer, curling and twisting up, up into the trees looking for food. When I walk near her, I am at once terrified and exhilarated, as if I am teetering on the edge of the world. Mandy rolls her trunk around now and takes an apple out of Desmona's hand.

"You see?" says Desmona. "Don't ask me questions. Don't even say anything. All that matters is that she's safe and happy right now. Don't you think?"

Actually, earlier this week when we were napping in the heat, we woke up and discovered Mandy was not tied to the tree anymore. Her rope had come loose, and she was gone.

Woolsey and Desmona started screaming, and I followed them down into the field. We ran along the edge of the woods until we came to an abandoned barn. It was Woolsey who discovered Mandy in the barn pulling down old bales of hay from an upper loft and eating away.

"That was a stroke of luck," said Riley when he found out about it later. And really it was, because Mandy needs huge amounts of food, and so we bring her over there at dusk when her great gray body blends with the dark sky, when the mist and gray of night come rolling over the field.

"It doesn't matter what we do next," says Desmona, stirring up the coals again so that the fire leaps up suddenly like an orange bird breaking out of a cage. "*This* is all that matters."

# Chapter Twenty-one

I'm not sure how late it is. The moon is low in the sky. This whole week it has been waxing toward a full moon. Oh, it's almost there tonight. When I look over at my sleeping friends, they look like alabaster statues flung around on the floor of the woods. My friends. I haven't ever been able to say that before. My friends.

Before I knew Desmona, I only had one friend, Mr. Krimms. My mother used to say, "What do you want to hang around with an old man for? You ought to have some friends your own age."

And I'd say, "I like his fish, and he has a whole wall full of stars in his apartment." Ever since I have known Mr. Krimms, he has always been there when I knock on his door. He's always there. I know he goes out to teach classes and I've seen him at Sage's and in the bookstore in the Square, but I've never, ever gone to his door and knocked and had him not answer.

"A friend is there when you need them," Mr. Krimms always says when he opens his door, "and a friend is forever."

I can remember how Mr. Krimms led me along through his apartment as if through mazes toward his piano, as if through mazes learning the world of music—first the notes, then the chords and scales, my right hand leaping one way, my left the other way, sewing it all together with my eyes on the music, my heart on the sound, the touch.

"A friend is there when you need them," he said, "and, Rachel, sometimes it is better, no, *necessary*, to talk about things, even things that you cannot bear to talk about. I have things, too, that I don't like to think of. You're not the only one."

Then Mr. Krimms told me how in Poland when the Gestapo came to his door, he and his wife started playing music. He went to the piano, and he began playing Mozart. His wife picked up her violin, and they played a duet together, louder and louder. Even as the Gestapo broke down their door, they were playing—harder, stronger. They kept it up, never stopping, never, until they were pulled away from their instruments, until they knocked Mr. Krimms's wife's violin to the floor. But they didn't break it. No, one of the guards grabbed it for himself, took it away in its case. They saw him outside as they were herded into a truck. They saw the officer hurrying down the street with a violin case under his arm.

"Never mind," said Mr. Krimms, "it was a long time ago, wasn't it? But you know, they hesitated. They hesitated, especially when we got to the crescendo. They paused. Isn't that something?"

"Yes," I said, "it is." I was sitting on the adjustable piano stool, spinning around and around as we talked, making the seat go way high and then spinning it back down low. But I was listening. I was picturing the Gestapo hesitating, being struck with awe by the presence of the music.

"What else in the world could make the Gestapo pause? Nothing," said Mr. Krimms.

*Sometimes it is necessary to talk about things.* A few years ago, I used to write little songs and Mr. Krimms used to play them for me. Once, he was so

taken with one little melody that he invited someone from the college to come over and hear it, and
he introduced me to him.

"It's rather remarkable, don't you think?" Mr.
Krimms said. But that was before, before I went to
Copley Square. Before I rode down, down almost
to the center of the world, lost in the crowd, lost in
the sea of people, lost in the sky of stars. Alone. After that, the songs went away. After that, I went to
school, and I didn't talk to anyone around me. I
was a moving target after that, a target in a gun ar-
cade, trying to get in and out of rooms at school
without getting noticed. Not one friend. Not a one.

That's when Desmona found me. She found me
just like she found Darcy and Woolsey and all the
others. Before she did, I used to see them moving
through the halls, Desmona in the lead, taller than
all the others. Pale little Darcy and Jacob B., all
the kids nobody wanted, surrounding her. Just
like the cats and dogs from the pound. Soon she'd
spotted me in the hall or on the stairs. Suddenly
they'd be there out of the blue, all of them.

"You're making friends," Mr. Krimms said to me
at one of my piano lessons.

"Well, sort of," I said, "in a way."

I look over at my friends now. I look over at

Mandy, who is lying by the big tree. Are her eyes closed? Her ears sweep forward like two big fans, and she seems to lift her trunk toward me as I look at her. Desmona is resting peacefully nearby on one of the couches. Her hair is tangled and full of twigs and hangs down onto the dusty ground around her. It's good that she's sleeping. She has gotten so tired.

Then I look around for Riley, and I see the other couch is empty. "Riley?" I call out. "Riley?" I get up off the pile of leaves and grass that I have made for a bed. I slip past Woolsey, who has rolled out of his tent and is curled up as tight as a ball in his sleep on the ground near the fire. It looks like you could roll him down a hill right now and he still wouldn't wake up.

"Riley?" I call again.

I make my way through the illuminated woods. The woods full of half-moon, three-quarter-moon light. Webbed dark branches, tiny stars, crunching sticks. "Riley?" I call. I get to the edge of the rise just beyond our campsite, and I look down into a leafy area below, which is full of strange soft shadows from the moon, and I can see Riley standing there, looking back at me. He's whistling the song "What a Little Moonlight Can Do" and he's wearing a necktie with his rumpled white T-shirt and squashed baseball cap.

"Riley? Where have you been?" I call.

And Riley goes, "Ssssh, I don't want you to wake my sister. She's sleeping, isn't she? She's completely exhausted," and he goes back to whistling "What a Little Moonlight Can Do."

"But where have you been?" I ask, and I go up to him and we stand in the darkness together.

"I can't stay with you guys all the time. You've got to understand that I have a life, too. Mickey O'Dell was having a party, so I went to play some piano for him. I had promised. I couldn't let him down. But I'm back now," says Riley.

As I look at him, he seems so haphazard in that necktie. Where did he get it? Just by the way his hat is tilted, I can tell right away Riley hasn't figured out what we should do about Mandy.

"But Riley," I say, "what about the elephant? What are we going to do?"

And Riley smiles at me and says, "You worry too much. We all need a good night's sleep, that's all."

I'm shivering as we stand there, not because it's cold exactly, but because it's night and I'm half asleep. Am I dreaming? Is there really an old circus elephant in the woods just behind me? Am I really standing so close to Riley McKarroll that I could fall against him?

Suddenly, Riley throws his arm over my back and says, "You're cold. Stop shivering. And stop worrying so much. You're just like Woolsey."

Then he smiles again, tilts his head, and starts whistling "What a Little Moonlight Can Do" as he walks back toward the campsite.

It's funny how things connect sometimes. My mom and I used to sing "What a Little Moonlight Can Do." It's a Billie Holiday song, and it used to be our favorite. When I was younger, we'd sing it together as we walked along the Charles River. At home we practiced lines over and over again to get it right so we could surprise my dad when he came in the door. We'd sing "What a Little Moonlight Can Do" when he came in all sooty and sweet from his workshop in the basement, and it always made him happy. Then he'd pantomime playing his saxophone, and we'd go singing around the living room, me in my stocking feet going for the back of the couch the way I always used to do, balancing and then slipping down into its softness, closing my eyes.

But then things changed. "They always do," said Mr. Krimms, and he pointed to one of his statues on a bookshelf—a carved wooden figure with a painted elephant head. "Ganesa," said Mr. Krimms, "the Indian god of protection during change. Look at his lovely painted head."

When I got older, my mom still sang with me, but somehow she wasn't really singing *with* me anymore. You could look at her and know she was somewhere else altogether, captivated, pulled by something invisible. What was it?

Riley is still singing now as he walks up the path. "What a Little Moonlight Can Do." Watching him walking through the woods, a realization comes to me. It washes over me like water on the ocean sand. *Was my mother feeling something for someone? Was it like the feeling I have right now for Riley McKarroll?*

After Riley leaves, I stand in the woods all alone with the sky above, strange and dark and mysterious and incomprehensible. Even the friendly names Mr. Krimms has given the stars do not make it any easier to look at them. Am I so small, so insignificant, so alone? How can I find a way out of this maze? The maze inside me and the maze we've made here by stealing this elephant and keeping her for so long in the woods? Who can help us? Not

Desmona, not Riley, not Woolsey, not Mickey, not Darcy . . . who? *Me?*

And then suddenly an idea floats out of me the way songs and music used to. I used to just feel them and write them down, and I couldn't believe how pretty they were. But then they stopped. Something stopped them, and no matter how hard I try, they won't come back.

Suddenly this little idea comes drifting up out of me just like that, just like a feather in the wind. And I grab it. And I turn around and run back up to the campsite. I grab my book bag. I get out a pen and paper, and I begin to compose a letter to the editors of the *Lockwell Times:*

> Dear sirs,
>
> It has come to my attention that the animals in Westwood Park Petting Zoo are being badly neglected, especially Mandy the elephant.

My pen seems to be flying over the paper. I go on to talk about the intelligence of elephants—their ability to love and care for one another, the way elephants stand in a circle around the little ones when there is danger, the way they mourn and cry when another elephant dies.

Yes, we have done something illegal. Yes, we have taken the elephant away into hiding, but we have only done this to capture your attention and to capture the attention of your readers, the good people out there who can perhaps change all this. We await your decision.

And I sign the letter:

Rachel Townsend
Desmona McKarroll
Riley McKarroll
and Alfred Pontiac III

# Chapter Twenty-two

When I look up from my paper, the stars are clear and bright. Desmona and Riley are still sleeping unaware in a forest full of shadows. Riley is completely motionless, lying on one of the ruined couches. He looks like Romeo, as if he too had taken some of the magic potion and had fallen asleep on a marble tomb. His red curls are carved in alabaster. His hand, lying open on the ground, holds nothing. Oh, Riley.

How can Desmona and Riley and Woolsey sleep when we've gotten into this terrible, unbelievable mess? I don't want to die. I've barely sprung to life. I don't want to live like Mary Queen of Scots in prison for all my young life, in prison the way Mandy was when we found her.

I reach again into my book bag and pull out an old Oreo cookie. My mother flickers across my mind again. She's putting on a hat with roses all over it. The roses are drooping. They have little faded faces on them. "Rachel," my mother once said about some flowers in the field, "look, they have little sad faces. You see that?"

I toss the cookie at Woolsey's rounded back. He's curled up like a chipmunk on a jacket. When the cookie hits, he bolts awake.

"Geeez, Rachel, kill me why don't you," he says.

"Woolsey," I say, "we have to do something. Look at them, aren't they like Hansel and Gretel? They're so innocent and unaware. They are made of nothing but dreams, *all dreams*. They don't even realize what we've done."

"Sheeesh," says Woolsey. "I'm so tired, I'm almost seeing double."

"We can't sleep now, Woolsey," I say. "We have to do something about this elephant. We're in a mess, Woolsey. Get your shoes on."

"What for?" he says.

Then I show Woolsey the letter I wrote. "It has to be hand-delivered," I say. "We don't have time to wait for the post office. We have to deliver this letter ourselves. It's our only hope. We have to make contact. Let them sleep. They might try to stop us."

Woolsey looks over at me with a reluctant bend in his neck, like a little boy who's late standing outside of a big school building, afraid to go in.

Woolsey and I head out through the long white dry grass. We quickly climb the small rise to Big Bill's Furniture Warehouse. We walk through it now, crunching broken glass under our feet, whispering. "The police could be anywhere out there. We have to be careful. If you see one, look away and look innocent. Look like you're just walking to school."

"Okay," says Woolsey, "but, I mean, a kid would have to be crazy to head out for school *this early.*"

I kind of keep an eye on Woolsey as we walk because he's somewhat unpredictable in a Woolsey sort of way. He does strange things that seem to come out of nowhere, which the social worker calls *manic.* Like the time we were walking in Harvard Yard and this old lady fell on the sidewalk in front of us. Then she couldn't get up, and we couldn't get her up. So Woolsey just sat down on the sidewalk with her and started telling her about his grandmother in Gary, Indiana, and how he and his father were going to move out there one of these days. Finally, the old lady got to her feet and tottered away. She was an art history professor at Harvard, and she liked Woolsey so much, she sent him a big copy of *Modern Traditions in Painting, Kandinsky to de Kooning*.

I don't know why Woolsey gets called manic by the social worker. I know Woolsey's big fear is that he won't grow any more, that he'll stay 4'9" forever. Most thirteen-year-olds grow. In fact, they all do, but tell that to Woolsey. Sometimes I've stopped in to see him in his apartment on the fourth floor and found him hanging upside down off his bed. "Don't say anything, Rachel," he said. "This is supposed to make you grow." Then we always end up talking about Napoléon and Bobby Zimmerman and how their height never kept them from great things.

Right now the highway is ahead of us. Once in a while a lonely truck swishes past, but mostly the road is silent. We scissor-hop over the metal guardrail and walk along the gravel headed into town, passing a Pandora sweater factory, which is lit up like a lantern in the dark. It must be the night shift.

Finally, Woolsey says, "Just where is the *Lockwell Times*, anyway, and while we're out here, what do you say to me calling my dad?"

"Don't worry about your dad, Woolsey," I say. "Don't forget, my dad stops in to have coffee with him every day. He'll take care of him."

"Yeah, but I'd still like to call him," says Woolsey.

"We can't make a phone call right now. It could be traced," I say.

"Yeah, but Mickey told me your parents are really scared, too. They've put up flyers all over the high school. He said everybody's pretty upset back at home. They're calling us runaways. I didn't actually intend to run away. Did you?"

I think for a second about this, and then I don't answer. I just let the warm night wind pull me along. We pass a big battered metal sign showing a dog putting mustard on a rusty hot dog. The sign says THE SALTY DOG SANDWICH SHOP and then CLOSED, MOVED TO 14 CARVER STREET. Pretty soon we come to a Dunkin' Donuts. The lights are on, and a couple of guys are hunched over the counter drinking coffee. What could bring them out so late?

We push open the door, moving carefully, as if we are walking over something invisible, something fragile and delicate. Inside, Woolsey nudges me, smiles, and says, "Let's load up on Bismarcks with maple glaze."

The guy at the counter goes, "So, Jean, had any elephants stop in for a cup lately?"

"No, by golly, but I had to walk home last night, and I was scared. I called Buzzy, but he was getting his beauty sleep and wouldn't give me a lift."

"No kiddin'?" says the guy. "And you could've been trampled. I heard he's a killer elephant. I heard he went berserk and busted out of there."

"Well, I wouldn't be so sure," says the waitress named Jean. "I used to go over there with my niece, and we used to pat that elephant."

"People are scared all over. They say the elephant went crazy ripping up trees and such," says the guy.

Woolsey puts a dollar on the counter. We get four maple Bismarcks and two cartons of milk.

Jean says to us, "You kids are up late."

"No," Woolsey says, "we're actually up early. We have a test at school today." Woolsey says this with such conviction, I almost believe him.

"Oh," says Jean, "you shouldn't be out there. Some animal has busted out of the zoo."

"We're just going to school," says Woolsey. And

we push out the door, both of us trying hard not to laugh, but finally we do. We break down laughing, spitting and spewing maple-glazed doughnuts all over the sidewalk.

A block away, we look back at the Dunkin' Donuts, and through the large lighted windows we see the waitress using the pay phone, gesturing and waving wildly as she talks.

A couple of streets over we see a police car with flashing lights. Then a city bus comes barreling up, doing its lonely rounds—no passengers at all riding in there. We flag it down, and it pulls up at its stop and we hop on. It's lit up as bright as a doctor's office in here. We climb into the lonely brightness, Lockwell flashing by now out the window like a dark, blurry dream. Woolsey and I rattle around to the back of the bus, like two pennies in a big empty piggy bank.

"Does this bus go to downtown Lockwell?" we ask.

"End of the line," says the driver, not really looking at us, as if he is in a dream, too, and doesn't want to be disturbed.

"Had any elephants for passengers?" says Woolsey, picking up on the Dunkin' Donuts man's joke.

Woolsey's not good at coming up with his own jokes, but he's good at revising material.

The bus driver laughs. Woolsey and I sit way at the back, the last seat in the house, for balance more than anything else.

In dark downtown Lockwell the bus opens its mouth like a big whale and out pop me and Woolsey on the sidewalk shivering like newborn puppies. The buildings, tall old skyscrapers, tower above us. Woolsey says, "Superman's city. Duh-de-dah." And he holds out his arms away from his cape, soaring through the sky.

"Woolsey," I say, "if this is Superman's city and we're headed for the newspaper office, you must be Jimmy Olsen, cub reporter."

"Baloney," says Woolsey. "Can't you see the wind in my cape?"

It's very, very dark. We pass gloomy-looking department stores, an elaborate but run-down movie theater with a Chinese pagoda theme, a Natick's hot dog place, a couple of pawnshops. Then we see the *Lockwell Times* building in the next block. There are lights on in the foyer. A janitor is pushing a wide broom through the hallway. We go to the door, knock. Woolsey puts his hands together like he's praying. The janitor comes to the door looking at us like he's trying to see through a curtain of disbelief.

"Oh, hello, sir," I say. I always fling the word *sir* around in these delicate situations. "Sir, could you help us? Please, sir?"

"What's the problem?" he says, opening the door.

"Could you give this very important letter with very important information to the editor in chief? Could you deliver it for us?"

The janitor looks at the letter. Then he looks back up and winks at us. "No questions asked," he says, smiling.

# Chapter Twenty-three

It took us about four hours to get back from town. We couldn't find a bus, so we had to walk the whole way. Now it's just becoming morning as we creep up the hill of rattling grass into the thin, shabby, dusty woods where we've been camping for over a week. At the top of the rise, I look back at Lockwell, and the sky is orange and radiant. Triumphant.

Woolsey and I are quietly excited and pleased, as if we both have a mouthful of birds that are singing, like the four and twenty blackbirds baked in a pie—that's Woolsey and me. We can't wait to say it, to tell Desmona and Riley what we've done. In all of our escapades, Desmona was the brave one, entirely in charge. But this time it's different. I feel a kind of perfect sureness. A sweet, pleasant, graceful sureness that absolutely no one can challenge right now. I set out to do something and I did it. It's done.

I think I was about ten years old when it first began to dawn on me that my mother wasn't always going to work when she went out saying she was. On the other hand, the idea didn't exactly surface overnight either. It was a slow realization, like a terrible fog lifting. At first I was too young to put the pieces together. I thought perhaps she was buying clothes all the time because she wanted to look as good as her customers at work. Well, of course, she had to set the example. But no, there was almost a hysteria about the way my mother shopped—a hunger, a longing, something I began to detect slowly.

When I was around eleven, she used to take me with her shopping. I would stand or sit with her in her dressing room and watch her fighting with awkward sleeves or flailing blindly under a tent of a skirt. It was when I watched her arms waving, unable to get in or out of some dress, that the understanding began to surface. My mother wasn't really with me at all. She was a million miles away. But if she wasn't here, where was she?

It was the day we brought tons of shopping bags home. They were all over the living room, full of shoes and purses, and there were new silk scarves trailing out of the bags like bright-colored snakes. My mother went into her room and came back out wearing one of her new outfits. Her new shoes squeaked and creaked on the wooden floor.

I sat on the couch pretending to read *The Life of Felix Mendelssohn*. I had actually already read that book. I had been wondering about his sister who also wrote music.

My mother's shoes creaked and squeaked across the living room and into the hallway, and then, with her new red purse swinging on her arm like a big pendulum, my mother went out the door. It clicked shut behind her. Locked tight. "I'll be back in a little while, sweetie," she called.

Sweetie. Sweetie. Sweetie. I put the book down. I leaned my head back on the couch. I didn't want to spend the afternoon reading a book I'd already read. I was eleven years old, and I decided to follow my mother when she went out that afternoon. And so I did. I rode the subway. I got on at Harvard Square just after she did. I stayed in the shadows. I was little and quick and quiet. I rode along one car behind her, *clickety-clack, clickety-clack.* Flickering subway lights. My mom in the next car looking out the window at the darkness, wearing a hat, a hat with small, sad roses. Up the stairs to cross the tracks. Down the stairs, changing trains. We got out at Copley Square—her first, then me, three or four people back, in among a string of businessmen. Four dark navy coats and a pair of red sneakers in the shadows. Me. Me following my mom, the subway trains screaming by in the tunnels underneath us, screaming, "Nooooooooo."

Copley Square was as bright as a coin. Eyes squinting. She went into Ken's Restaurant smiling, little roses on her hat lilting, dipping. She found a booth. I was there, too, three booths back. I was peering over. My mom was sitting with a man. He was like a husband. They were kissing, a long slow kiss. My mom was crying. The man was crying, too. They kissed again and again. He was her husband, but what about my father? The man was buying things—flowers, cheesecake, champagne, candy. The flowers leaned over, crying into the table. *Nooooooo.* My mother and the man were eating Boston cheesecake, and I wondered at the time why they weren't having banana cream pie, which is what I would have ordered, bananas being my very favorite. *Noooooooooooo.*

Woolsey and I sit down at the top of the hill, waiting for the sun to creep up over the factories and warehouses of Lockwell, Massachusetts. We can see pinkness starting to form along the horizon. I look at Woolsey, whose face seems soft in the early light, and yet he looks more grown-up, more sure than he's looked to me before.

And suddenly it just pours out of me. I tell him. I tell him about my mother, how I saw her kissing another man, a man who was not my father. I tell him how I rode home alone on the subway frozen inside, frozen on a hot summer day.

Then we hear something in the field below. We look down and realize it's Riley, Riley running in the dawn light, leaping like a great long-legged deer. He's got a newspaper in his hands, and he's waving it wildly and shouting, "You're not gonna believe this. They printed a letter. It's on the front page. You're never gonna believe this."

# Chapter Twenty-four

As the sun finally comes above the horizon, the field lights up with warm, brilliant, direct sunlight, casting the whole industrial area in an eerie golden glow. Suddenly the pond seems to be made of yellow light, and Big Bill's Furniture Warehouse is transformed, almost dreamlike—floating on the grass like a castle bathed in all this sunshine.

We wake Desmona up because down in the field among the milkweed stands and the sunlight are migrating swarms of monarch butterflies. There are hundreds of them fluttering and rising, fluttering and rising. I can't really believe my eyes. There are so many of them.

Maybe it's because we're so exhausted, but it is while we are looking at the butterflies that we all start laughing. We laugh and laugh and laugh. And then Riley comes toward me with his long flannel arms and gives me a hug because it's such a sight, and I feel as if I am made of light and soaring butterflies.

Then we look a little closer, and we see swarms of police cars, dozens of them, flashing and blinking at the edge of the field. The police are getting out of their cars, and they are coming toward us with guns, a whole army of them.

For some reason, Mandy knows they're coming. She begins pulling on her rope and rocking back and forth. Then she screeches and trumpets.

Woolsey is shaking. "What am I supposed to do, Desmona? Tell me what to do."

"I don't know, Woolsey," she says. "I don't know." She's crying. Desmona is shivering and crying.

Riley is perched the closest to them, crouching behind the corrugated metal fence we constructed. But Desmona is collapsing. She seems to be making no sense. "Mommy," she cries. "Mommy, where are you? Where are you? I'm scared, Mommy." Desmona is sobbing, and her words are garbled.

Riley leaves his post and puts his arms around

Desmona. "Des," he says. "Des, come back, come back."

Everybody is falling to pieces around me. The troopers are getting closer. They're now at the foot of the incline at the edge of the field. I just keep noticing how there are these butterflies everywhere, and it seems so strange and sad.

The troopers stop and form a line around the little hill where we are. One trooper takes his gun out of his holster and shoots at the sky. Then he raises a bullhorn to his mouth and speaks into it. "This is State Trooper Robert G. Mills. Cease and desist. I repeat, cease and desist. We have you surrounded. Are you armed? If so, throw down your weapons. We know you have the elephant. It is a dangerous wild animal. Please release it now. Please release it now."

I look to Riley and Des. Riley is still cradling Desmona. She's still sobbing. They seem barely aware of the state trooper's request. They didn't seem to hear him. Woolsey, too, looks pale and lost standing behind a small tree.

It takes me it seems years to move. I feel I'm in a dream, where it takes me forever to run, to reach for something—even to speak. I see Riley's bullhorn lying on the ground. I want to reach for it, but everything is so slow, so sluggish. I lean over. I feel like I'm going to fall. Then I grab the metal bull-horn, get my hands around it. How heavy it is. I raise it to my mouth and speak into it, trying not to cry.

"State Trooper Robert Mills, my name is Rachel Townsend. I am thirteen years old. This is a protest. We want better conditions for this gentle, lovely elephant. We want *much* better conditions."

As we are led through the field of tall grass and bright late-morning sunlight, there are lines of re-porters and police and crowds of people. Many of them are carrying posters and signs that say SAVE THE ELEPHANT and MANDY, WE LOVE YOU. My letter printed in the *Lockwell Times* this morning must have reached them. There are hundreds of people cheering and clapping as we walk by in handcuffs—Mandy in the lead with ropes and chains and a wreath of lilacs around her neck.

# Chapter Twenty-five

Freedom is certainly a state of mind, proven by the fact that I feel freer than I've ever felt in all my thirteen years tonight in the Lockwell City Jail. Riley and Des and Woolsey and me are all lying on cots in one cell. The cell next to us is empty.

They've been really nice to us actually. Yesterday the policeman on duty brought us dinner from the sandwich shop across the street. He even took our orders like a waiter with a pad, but in his hat and uniform, he looked like he was writing up a traffic ticket. We had grilled cheese sandwiches that tasted so incredibly good since we hadn't eaten anything except apples and cookies for over a week. After the policeman took our orders, Riley started calling him *garçon. Hey, garçon, can I go to the can?*

They even pushed the *Lockwell Evening News* through the bars a while ago, and the four of us have been sitting here looking at ourselves and Mandy on the front page. It seems they reprinted my letter, and many people have written in letters, too, cheering and agreeing with us. The article says that people have donated large amounts of money and that an important animal rights group has called the newspaper. They are talking about plans to send Mandy to a large open-air zoo where she will have space to roam. We kind of cried for joy when we read that.

So here we are feeling tired and free. I feel like anything in the world is possible now, like I can do anything I want if I just make a plan.

Riley and Des are really involved in the idea of being in jail. Riley's playing his harmonica, which resonates off the walls in a special way. Riley says harmonicas and the blues can't come into their own until they're played in a jail. The echo and tone, he says, isn't quite right anywhere in the world but here. He's been happily wailing away for hours.

Des takes this very seriously, lying on her cot

looking out through the bars with tears pouring down her cheeks. She says she's thinking of all the prisoners who have been here before. And then we all sing "We Shall Overcome," which is what people have been singing recently in jails in the South.

After supper, I sit on the floor listening to the echoing harmonica, reading all the messages scratched and written on the wall—names, mostly, and dates. The oldest being *1918, Jediah Smotes.* A more recent one says, *Bubbles, I'm coming home.*

Desmona looks over at me. She says, "Gretchen will probably be here in the morning, and I'm dreading it. I'm guessing she'll use this as a means to push me into going to prep school. And in some ways, having done this, I might be willing. I might be ready to go now. Oh, Rachel," she says, "I'm sorry about pooping out on you when they came for us. I didn't know I would fall to pieces like that. I sort of want to thank you for getting that letter to the newspaper, too. I'm so sorry I let you down."

"You didn't let me down, Desmona. Far from it," I say, looking at that graffiti—*Bubbles, I'm coming home.*

# Chapter Twenty-six

When my father drives the rented car up to the curb, everything seems different. Eighty-seven Brattle Street is a different building. It's a different street. The sky is a different blue. The trees were full of pale green spring leaves when we left, and now, eleven days later, the leaves are a dark summer green.

My father drives away to return the rented car, and I walk by myself back into the tall brick horseshoe-shaped apartment building. Right away I notice there is too much wind in the hallway. Doors are open that shouldn't be. The door to Mr. Krimms's apartment, number 1A, in particular. Why is the door ajar? There is a hollow echoey sound emanating from the rooms beyond. A feeling of space and light comes through the open door like wind.

"Mr. Krimms," I call, and when I push open the door, sunlight and silence falls on all his furniture — the couch covered in tiny Indian mirrors, his quiet, waiting books, his wooden carvings. What is all this lightness and silence, this sunlight? Suddenly I feel angry at the space and sunlight. Why is it here? It has never been here before.

"Mr. Krimms," I shout. "What's going on?" I run from room to room, stopping short in front of the butterfly lily, which has bloomed its glorious bloom, the one we waited so long to see. It's orange with a black stripe, like a monarch butterfly. "Mr. Krimms," I shout, "the butterfly lily — it's a monarch. It bloomed!"

I run past his African teakwood table, the painted statue of the elephant Ganesa, the wall-hanging from Egypt, the huge brass vase full of dried lavender from southern France.

Then I see the great blue globe sitting there, full of silence. There is a note taped to it. It says, *This is for you, Rachel. The world is yours.*

I sit in a corner crumpled down as small as a rock, and I start shivering. "Mr. Krimms," I call out again, and it echoes in this windy, silent apartment. Then I notice the fish tank, and I see all the rare species in there floating together making bubbles. "Mr. Krimms," I call again, and I start to cry.

Someone comes out of the kitchen carrying Mr. Krimms's toaster. She says she is Mr. Krimms's cousin. I have never in all my life seen such a completely horrible, awful, dreadful person.

I run into a small back room, and I slam the door and lock it. Then I lie down on the floor and cry and cry. I stay in here for hours. I won't come out. I'm never leaving this room.

My mother comes to the door and knocks. "Rachel," she says, "open the door, honey. Don't cry. Mr. Krimms was an old, old man. Don't cry."

"Go away," I shout. "Go away. You lied to me. I saw you in Copley Square at Ken's Restaurant. I saw you. I know what you did."

By evening I go upstairs to my room. I feel weak, and I lean against the wall for support. When I walk into my room, I feel like I'm in a different place. The room smells of fresh paint. The walls are yellow. There is a fluffy new yellow bedspread on the bed, and there is a bouquet of big yellow flowers on the dresser. The window is open, and the warm Cambridge air blows in.

My mother is standing in the door. She has a tiny spot of yellow paint on her arm. She's looking down at her hands. She has something to tell me, but she hasn't got any way to say it. Her hands look like they are about to move, to make words, to sign as if I were deaf. But I'm not deaf. I know what she's trying to say as she looks down at her hands. She doesn't have to make her voice shape the words.

"Rachel, I should have told you sooner. We need to talk about your father and me and our plans for divorce." After a while, my mother comes over to me and gives me a hug. "I'm sorry, honey," she says. "I'm so sorry. I'm so sorry about everything. But did you know that one of the last things Mr. Krimms said was that he wanted this brought upstairs for you. Do you know what Mr. Krimms left you?"

And I shake my head no.

"Well, you didn't see it then," she says. "It's just behind you."

And I turn around, and there is Mr. Krimms's piano in the corner, sitting in my room.

## Chapter Twenty-seven

Spring turned into summer very quickly, the way it does some years. It's almost winter now, and all those delicate green leaves have turned orange and fallen away into the wind. My parents are getting a divorce, and I have begun riding the Green Line to Newton every weekend, where my mother has a little house with a yard. But I still spend most of my time at 87 Brattle Street, visiting the Butterfield sisters, visiting Woolsey and Sergeant Pontiac.

By the way, Riley McKarroll kept his promise to Woolsey about that Red Sox game. On a beautiful warm summer day, he pulled up in a big station wagon beeping the horn. He was wearing a baseball cap, and Desmona was, too. Their stepmother was sitting in the backseat, and I was surprised when she said hello to me.

Riley was hopping around, so excited that he didn't even take the elevator in our building, but leaped up the long narrow staircase to the fourth floor to Sergeant Pontiac and Woolsey's apartment. We wheeled the sergeant to the elevator, and then my father and Riley lifted him into a chair that was positioned in there. We took him down to the ground level and then lifted him back into his wheelchair.

When we got him out to the car and Sergeant Pontiac saw Desmona's stepmother, he said, "Good afternoon to you. This is my son, Alfred. My son, Alfred, was away for a long time, but he's back now."

"Come on, Dad," said Woolsey, "we can sit in the front seat." And then he looked at Desmona and said, "I called shotgun way back at the elevator."

Finally, we all drove off to the Red Sox game, and it was almost a perfect day, except that the Red Sox lost. Halfway through the fourth inning, I turned around and noticed an almost happy look on Sergeant Pontiac's face.

That was really the last time I got to do anything

much with Desmona and Riley. Well, their step-mother wouldn't let Desmona out of her sight through most of June and July and August.

I did see Riley one more time during the summer. He had gotten really thin, and he was slouching the way Riley slouches in the easy chairs in the Radcliffe Center across the street. I happened to be walking through there one day to get to the courtyard and there he was. His eyes were hollow-looking, and he kept ripping a paper cup into pieces as we talked. It was still about Christina. I don't think I've ever seen anyone so lovesick — except for me, except for the way I feel about Riley.

We sat and talked for a while, me suggesting that he might invite her on a date. And Riley saying no he could never, ever risk her rejecting him. He couldn't be sure. He would be destroyed if she turned him down. He had to be sure.

So I looked at Riley Red for the last time. I looked at his jazz piano hands. Those same hands could wrap around a pool cue and clean up. Those same hands could pick a lock. Except for his fear of telephones and rejection, he was near perfect. He granted his sister all her wishes. He owned the world. He was the world — but he could never love me. I turned and looked at my Riley Red, and then I got up and walked away.

That night it was hot out. I opened my window and looked at Cambridge in the night. The sound of crickets sang in the darkness, reminding me of the night Desmona insisted we all run out in our pj's to Henry Wadsworth Longfellow's house and pick cherries in the great cherry tree in his yard.

"We can make Henry Wadsworth Longfellow cherry preserves with those cherries," she said. "And we'll give a jar to Burns. We'll make labels with pictures of laughing Allegra and Edith with the golden hair."

And so we did. We ran in the soft spotlights in the shadow of the great yellow house on Brattle Street. We got enough cherries for five jars of Henry Wadsworth Longfellow cherry preserves, and it was scrumptious.

It was a night like *that* when I opened the window and sat at my desk and let my curtains loose to move in the wind. It was a night like *that* that I wrote another letter. This one was to Riley. It said, *Dear Riley, I noticed you when you visited Commonwealth School this spring on visiting day with Mickey O'Dell. Please call me—I'd love to talk. My number is 555-0952.* And I signed the letter, *Love, Christina Talbot.*

Why did I write that letter? Why? Some people may think I was a complete idiot to ruin my chances with the only boy I've ever loved in my short thirteen years. But the truth is, I loved him so much that I wanted him to have what he so desperately needed. I could not bear to see Riley McKarroll suffering. And so I wrote the letter, knowing that was the only way that Riley would get up the nerve to call Christina. And his love for her was so beautiful that I loved even his love for her. I love, loved, every inch of Riley McKarroll.

And after I had done it, and Riley had called Christina and they had gone out on a date, I was rewarded in a funny kind of a way. It started when I was riding the elevator, the up, up, up motion. I went into my room, and I was tinkering with the notes on Mr. Krimms's piano when I began to hear it. I listened and I heard it clear and defined, the piano notes, the chords and themes—the whole thing. Slowly I began to play the sweet, lilting, dreamy melody that I was hearing in my head. My hands were trembling, and I had tears in my eyes as I realized I was playing my own music. When I had written it down on many sheets of paper, I called my first real piece of music *Sonata #1 for Riley Red*.

Over the course of the rest of the summer, I tried to call Desmona many times, but I only got the housekeeper, who said she was not in. Still, I wanted to thank Desmona. I wanted to say *thank you*, so I went over there one day and knocked on the huge front door, but no one answered. I looked up at Desmona's windows — no curtains drawn, no shades pulled, only blankness. I stood out in the yard for a while. Everything was silent except for the wind in the trees and some wind chimes slinging together somewhere out of sight. As I was leaving, I noticed that Desmona had forgotten the death mask of e. e. cummings underneath the bushes. It was still lying there among the grass and leaves, smiling. I stood there a moment, and I kind of smiled back.

Then, out of the blue about a week later, I got a postcard from Desmona. Maybe someone had seen me in her yard after all. It said, *Dear Rachel, I'll be going to Pond Hill Academy on August 29th in the morning.* And then she added, *One great deed. One glorious contribution. We did it! Love, Desmona.*

They say good things come out of bad things. Well, Sergeant Pontiac and Woolsey were able to move to apartment 1A on the ground floor by the end of June. And since then, Sergeant Pontiac has been able to get out on the street every day in his wheelchair.

And no one claimed the fish and the fish tank, so when Woolsey moved in, they became his, and I think it has changed his life. He has gotten very interested in the fish and in biology and now plans to go to college. He has grown three inches since summer and has let his fawn-brown hair grow soft and long below his ears.

Since they have moved to the first floor, Woolsey has had no need to worry about his father, Sergeant Pontiac. My father always takes good care of him, bringing him for a daily trip in his wheelchair down into Harvard Square to the newspaper stand to buy the *New York Times*, passing all the Cliffy girls walking out of Radcliffe Yard, passing the ninety-two-year-old Butterfield sisters with their net bags of groceries leaving Sage's, or the white-haired professor's wife with a feather in her hat and a parrot perched on her shoulder. Sergeant Pontiac has become a kind of fixture in Harvard

Square, telling everyone every day about the burning, blazing, sunlit beaches of Normandy, France.

By this fall, too, the Beatles' music came to America, and suddenly everyone in the world has long hair. Not just Desmona and me and Riley, but the whole world. And Desmona isn't the only one to protest anymore—everyone is protesting. But I swear we were the very first ones.

Desmona went off to boarding school this fall as she promised she would, leaving behind her eight to ten cats and dogs saved from death and placed in good homes, a yard full of cardinals, an elephant rescued from a life worse than death and moved to a large open-air zoo, and a good handful of friends deemed losers, leftovers, left-outs—myself included—changed forever.

Desmona McKarroll, fighter for the poor, the left-out, fighter against injustice, ready to give it all up—her money, her stature, her life—for her cause. We were her cause.

On that early fall morning when she went off to boarding school, Desmona got in her father's black limousine with her hair in a tight bun—no eye shadow under her eyes—her feet in brown oxfords.

Woolsey and I waited on the marble benches outside the Cambridge Performance Center to see her go by, to wave to our friend Desmona, and I hoped then, and I hope now, that she has the strength of spirit to endure, to hold on, and maybe even to grow and bloom like the cherry blossoms in Henry Wadsworth Longfellow's beautiful garden.